D1527351

A SPOT OF

EARL

SLAY

TEA TIME TROUBLES

BOOK 1

AUBREY ELLE

Disclaimer

This is a work of fiction. Names, characters, businesses, places, events, and incidents are either the products of the author's imagination or used in a fictitious manner. Any resemblance to actual persons, living or dead, or actual events is purely coincidental.

Editing: Expressions Editing; C.J. Pinard at
www.cjpinard.com
Proofreading: PSW
Cover: Donna Rogers at
www.dlrcovercoverdesigns.com

Chapter One

December was inarguably the busiest month of the year, but I couldn't imagine delaying this move a single day. I was past-due relocating as it was. With every mile I drove my seventeen-year-old daughter further from her hometown, another knot of tension seemed to relax from my shoulders.

"You're doing it again," Ella lectured from the passenger seat, not even glancing up from her phone.

Caught, I paused mid-roll in rotating my shoulders. Peeved at her mothering *me*, I refrained from letting her catty tone distract me. Eyes on the road—and traffic wasn't that bad—I sighed and slumped into the driver's seat. Heaven forbid she catch me not looking forward. She had yet to gain the desire for her driver's license, but my, oh, my, she was an expert at backseat driving.

"Haven't had time for yoga lately," I admitted. While she *was* nagging me, noticing my visible display of tension as I drove us to this new beginning in the small, rural town of Fayette, I liked to think she pointed out my flaws out of love and maybe worry for me, not scolding.

"Uh-huh." She flicked her long brown hair back as she swiveled in her seat to directly face my profile. "But why *are* you so tense? Skipping yoga or not, I would think you'd be happier now." She gifted me her signature scoff before adding, "I mean, *one* of us should be giddy with all these life-altering changes."

Ah, okay. This time, it wasn't love, worry, or scolding. Just another offering of her scorn. *Lucky me!*

I pulled my lips into my mouth, clamping down on them to keep my honesty in. Depending on the moon cycle, the grace of Karma, and who knows, the weather, her attitude would either simmer and she'd get over it, or I was in for a long earful. Bottom line, I had no control over her mood swings. I almost winced, thinking back to all those times I'd given my mother a hard time during my adolescence.

What goes around, comes around, Naomi...

Regardless, I was convinced it was better not to reply to her bait.

"The high school doesn't even have a debate team, Mom!"

I tilted my head to the side, spotting the *Welcome to Fayette* sign I sped by. "Pretty sure you could start up your own, El. Open your mouth, and whatever someone replies *will* be a debate."

"Are you trying to say I'm antagonistic?" she retorted.

"That'd be a magnanimous way of putting it."

She raised her arms, giving me jazz hands as she rolled her eyes. "Oooh. Big word, Mom."

"All the better to charm you."

"But seriously—"

"But seriously," I cut in as I obeyed the navigation screen ordering me to turn left. "We've gone over this. The fact Fayette High School lacks a debate team is a blow to you, I know this, and I'm sorry about it, but it's not something I can control."

She crossed her arms and slumped, facing forward again. "You can control us moving here."

"No, I can't. And you know it." Snow fell faster than the fluffy, light flurries we'd been traveling through, almost as though the precipitation matched my daughter's ire. I flicked the wipers to sweep across the windshield faster. "Right?"

No reply.

Since September, we had discussed this thoroughly. But I guessed Ella hadn't achieved an adult-like capacity to *accept* it yet. My only hope was that one day, she would stop bemoaning it.

After a patience-seeking sigh, I reminded her. "We're moving *here* because my uncle Fred left me his house." In other words, it was the only place we'd be able to afford as I embraced my newly divorced lifestyle—and finances.

She huffed, looking out her window. Yep. She was aware.

"And we're moving because neither of us could tolerate living in Swenton anymore." Not with the way her father was handling the end of our marriage.

"But something you *can* control is making a debate team at your new school," I suggested. "Right?"

She remained quiet.

"Why worry or complain about what you can't control and—"

"Focus on what you can." She tacked a groan to the end of it. "Yes. I *have* heard that before, thank you very much." As she ran her fingers through her hair, fluffing it up stylishly to give it some lift, she slanted her shoulder to press it against the window. "I guess I can be happy about moving here for one reason."

Oh, praise be. One *reason?* Was that optimism blooming now? "Yeah? What's that?"

"Not living in Swenton means you won't go to therapy with Dad anymore."

Hallelujah. I hadn't enjoyed a single second of that so-called marriage counseling, but it was handy for a third party to confirm staying married was a lost hope. Almost like verification of *I told you so* to my ex and my ex-mother-in-law.

"Which means I shouldn't have to put up with you regurgitating little mantras like that all the time."

I grinned, catching her smirk in my peripheral vision. "Like only concern yourself with what you can control?" I nodded. "Yeah, your dad *hated* when I said that, too." I'd only parroted what the counselor advised. If he couldn't control his desire to cheat on me, then I couldn't control my "inability" to love him anymore. I wondered if I ever had.

Good grief. And good riddance.

Ella's giggle suggested her annoyance with me had cooled, and I reached over to pat her hand. "It'll get better. You know, this isn't for good."

She shot me a look of alarm, pencil-thin brows arching high. "You mean we might go back to Swenton someday?"

Heck, no! "I mean we're moving here for now." As the words left my lips, I watched the scenery blur by. This main street was quaint and cutesy in its own way, but it lacked the bustle and energy of the bigger small town we'd left.

Shops and a café stood between the usual establishments. Post office, bank, a mom-and-pop shoe store, and a couple of dinky little bars. In one minute, we traversed the bulk of Fayette and it *was* slightly underwhelming. Dare I think it—boring.

I wasn't moving us here blindly. I'd looked it up. Fayette didn't have much fame to claim. The last edition of their local newspaper bragged about a teacher who competed in all 5ks for charity. Some commercial bakery had gone through yet another buy-out. A dry cleaner had won an award for something, entrepreneurship excellence. A lady was lucky winning the state lotto… Usual, small-town news.

Scrolling on social media didn't give me the impression Fayette would be an unwise choice for a new start in life. Some teen, Varga somebody, had gotten another underage DUI. Worrisome, but Ella didn't gravitate to bad boys, or boys at all yet. A woman with an ID picture of cats on her shoulders complained about how the town should clear snow off all residential sidewalks and only use pet-safe ice melts. I'd paused, rereading a report from the police chief about a string of thefts from older citizens' homes. That did sound worrisome, but I hoped our new house would be in a safe end of town. Thefts could happen anywhere.

"But that doesn't mean we can't move somewhere else later, as we see fit."

"More like when your bank account sees fit," Ella sassed.

I shrugged, seeing no reason to be ashamed of the truth. As perceptive as Ella was, it was nothing to hide from her. She was witness to her father sabotaging my attempts of employment, criticizing my desire for even a part-time job. He'd often accused me of belittling the family name, that wanting to work would render us too middle class and thus make a mockery of him. He was loaded, but I saw through his manipulative words at the divorce proceedings. If I fought for adequate child support and alimony, he'd demand a ridiculous mishmash of shared custody. When I said I didn't want his money, he'd quickly changed his tune to *get lost*. We'd settled on the bare minimum he should have paid, but it was a *teeny* savings that gave me the confidence to believe Ella and I could start a new life here.

"And that shouldn't be long. Our finances won't stay so…"

"Pathetic?"

I furrowed my brow. "Hey, there are plenty of people with less in the world. Be grateful."

"I am. I am. I'm grateful I've got you."

Awww. I smiled at her. "And I've got you. Our finances won't be this limited for long. Just until paychecks come in."

"From what job?" she challenged.

"I'm sure I'll find something."

"Where?" Ella waved her hand at the window. "There's nothing here!"

We'd already driven through the main part of town, and according to the navigation, we were minutes from our new home. Overall, from what we'd seen so far, Fayette didn't strike me as a hopping, bustling place that might be overflowing with job vacancies.

"I'll find something somewhere. Even remote. We'll make it work."

"This whole place is remote," she said as we passed another farm.

"Maybe. But it's practically free. Somewhere to get our bearings until we find something better."

Especially since Uncle Fred left me the house already. Not worrying about a mortgage was a godsend. And how much could utilities be in this little town? There was no social life to enjoy, so I'd be saving there as well.

"Yeah, but what if this *free* house is, like, dilapidated and musty and broken, and…" She shuddered. "You know? You get what you pay for?"

"It hasn't been sitting there empty for too long," I confessed. Uncle Fred was more of a distant relative, but I was pretty sure I'd met him, oh, twenty years ago at my First Communion. Him leaving me the house was a surprise, and I suspected he'd only done so because he had no other family to consider.

"Besides," I said drolly, sneering at the windshield as I turned onto our street, "your grandparents insisted on checking out the most recent listing of it to ensure I wasn't moving you to an 'inhumane hovel unsuitable for residence.'"

This time it was Ella's turn to pat my thigh in sympathy. "I don't know how you ever put up with them, Mom."

"Oh, it took some practice, all right."

With excitement building faster, I pulled into the driveway and set the truck in park. I raised my hand, brandishing it toward the two-story brick house. "But now, we're free from those meddling, impossible-to-please relatives. Tada! Home, sweet home!"

Ella scrunched her nose as she stared at the nondescript house. I looked my fill too, never having seen it aside from a few images on my phone.

Wind whistled outside, and the strong current shook the maple tree to the right of the front porch. Bare branches jerked and whipped until bark cracked. A long length of wood crashed on the front yard already littered with twigs and sticks. Tall grass and weeds added to the miserable lack of curb appeal. Stuck in clumps of dead grass were flyers and advertisements that had escaped the screen door.

"You get what you pay for…" Ella muttered.

And we were getting a hand-out, all right. I couldn't help but wince.

At least the house seemed solid. The roof was intact, windows weren't busted, and the porch wasn't sporting missing rails. Structurally, it would do, but as far as a sense of welcoming us in?

"The house inspector said it was livable."

Ella shot me a stern look. "At what minimum?"

"Well, it'll be up to us to make it homey, then." I gently swatted her, more than tired of her attitude after the nine-hour drive. "Come on. I didn't raise you to be a whiny brat."

And I sure hope your dad didn't mold you to be materialistic despite my best efforts. I couldn't deny the comparison. Back in Swenton, we'd lived in a well-maintained, ostentatious mansion built to impress, not to house a loving family. Ella hadn't wanted for anything, nearly spoiled with any gift or trip she'd dreamed of.

"Hey. I'm not whining." She frowned, but I caught a hint of shame in her tone. "Just…observing."

I snorted my sentiments at her observations. "Well, we're gonna make do with what we have."

"Okay, okay. We will. You and me, together against the world. Rah." She reached for her door handle as I did for mine. "It's just…"

"An empty, uninviting house." I exited the truck and zipped up my coat. There was no point lying about it.

She slammed her door shut and nestled into her coat and scarf, nodding in a new turn of brightness. "So the faster we get inside and liven it up, the bet—"

Another branch fell under the December wind. It busted onto the sidewalk, splintering into smaller sticks and twigs in a mess.

"Okay." I rounded the truck and draped an arm around Ella's shoulders, pulling her closer to me as I eyed the ancient tree shedding before our eyes. "First on the list, find a company to trim that tree."

"And invest in hard hats."

I smiled at Ella. "Funny. It can't be windy like this all the time." I was sure the tree was just neglected as the rest of the yard had been before Fred died. "Hop back in. I'll pull up to the back door so we can avoid an injury."

She didn't need telling twice. We escaped the brutal bite of the wintry wind, climbing into the truck. I started the engine again, biting my lip at the loud groan. A glance to my left showed a curtain flicking back into place from the next house's window.

Oh, great. Already being a loud nuisance for the neighbors…

I drove further up the drive and turned off the rental truck once more. No tall trees waited in the backyard, and the sidewalk to the back door was clear of the abundance of debris the front had. With a privacy fence sheltering a portion of the lawn back here, the clear path made more sense.

Once more, we exited the moving truck, both of us shivering at the contrast from the toasty warmth of the vehicle to the chill brushing at us outside.

"Hurry. Let's get in and turn on the furn—"

Ella stopped me though, her hand on my sleeve. A loud clap of wood on wood startled me, and I jumped. She dropped her arm and pointed.

A shed stood in the rear corner of the yard, its double doors wide open, waving to and fro in the wind.

"We should probably close those, first," Ella said. Again, the door on the left flung back, and we both jerked and winced at the sound of the wood smacking. Unlike the house, the shed was made of old, once-red, weathered planks.

"Good idea. Before the doors fly off altogether," I agreed. Even though I wasn't sure about staying in Fayette for long, we would be here for now. And letting doors get carried away in the wind to be deposited elsewhere as trash didn't seem like an impressive way to arrive.

We wrapped our arms around ourselves, bundled into our coats the best we could as we hurried toward the shed. Wind still whipped at our faces in the ten-yard dash, and my eyes watered while my nose stung from the cold.

"Brr…" I exaggerated as I reached out to grip the edge of the door.

Ella braced the opposite door with her foot, so it wouldn't fling into her face. But when she pressed her hand against the feeble panel, she couldn't close it completely.

"Go on, close it. Then I can latch this hook to lock them."

She shook her head, using both hands to shove the door shut. Weird. For as easily as they were waving open, back and forth in the wind, I would have guessed the hinges would go smoothly.

"I can't. It won't shut."

I stepped closer, holding my door so it wouldn't strike me. "Huh?"

As I pulled the thin wood back, opening the entrance, I stumbled. I sucked in a breath of icy air.

"What? What is it?" Ella demanded after my gasp. She nudged closer, but I raised my arm to barricade her from peering inside.

Too late.

She shrieked, clutching my sleeve as she spotted the lifeless body sprawled near the threshold.

AUBREY ELLE

Chapter Two

Nightfall crept closer, and the winds only dug in for the evening. Shivering, both from the December weather and the shock of finding a corpse in the shed out back, Ella and I huddled into our coats as we stood off to the side.

I'd called the police as soon as I ushered her back, and the cavalry showed up quite quickly. To Ella's snark, I had to agree it should have taken them no time at all. "In a dinky little town this small, where else are they going to be?"

As I gave the address to dispatch, I'd been careful to reiterate no one was out and about as far as we could tell, but the kindly woman instructed us to wait in a safe location. We'd chosen the moving truck instead of heading into the house, for no other reasons than we'd become familiar with that rental vehicle, and it *felt* safer than entering the house for the first time.

"Just go on back in the truck, El," I told my daughter as she bounced in her step to keep warm. I wasn't sure I even needed to be standing out here anymore. I'd spoken with the Fayette Police Chief, a cop, or two, or three. Their bulky winter outer coats were too similar in dark brown, and with nearly matching hats and gloves covering more of them up, I couldn't spot too many features to distinguish one from the other. I couldn't offer much information, but I provided the details I did have, few as they were. For the last hour, they'd spent the bulk of their time at the shed and collaborating with the techs from the forensic van that had pulled up in the alley behind the property—closer to the shed.

They hadn't outright granted me permission to leave yet. And where would I go, anyway? Nor had they directly asked me to stick around. I remained standing outside as a courtesy, I supposed. My worry was that it would seem rude or suspicious if I tried to leave the scene. One officer had asked to check out the house, just in case anyone was loitering, and after I unlocked the back door and gestured for him to have it at, I resumed my post with Ella in the driveway.

"What would sitting in the truck do?" Ella asked, her teeth chattering.

"Oh, I don't know. Some warmth? Ward off hypothermia."

She rolled her eyes at me. "It's not *that* cold." Yet she proved it was a lie as she tightened her scarf around her neck.

"El, just—"

"I don't want to," she said instead. "I don't want to miss anything."

I flung an arm up, silently asking *miss what?* It wasn't like the cops were interviewing me and could ask for her input.

"Mooney!" a woman yelled, her bold voice loud enough over the steady wind whistling in the air.

I leaned to see past Ella on my left, spotting a short woman sticking her head out from the side door of the neighboring house. Deep, rich auburn curls of her retro perm stayed firm against the breeze. Scowling toward the shed, she didn't seem too happy about the crowding arrival of Fayette's law enforcement crew. She wore a hot pink sweatshirt with tight jeans, but the black apron covering her front was more than dusted and dirtied with flour and tan smears. Perhaps we'd interrupted a peaceful baking time.

"Mooney!" she hollered again, propping a hand at her hips as she stepped out further from her open door.

Who was Mooney? I couldn't recall the cops' names. I wanted to cringe, realizing our entrance to

Fayette's community would be one tainted with trouble.

"Chief," one of the forensic techs said, chuckling lightly.

From the shed, a lean man strolled out, his face sporting weariness, his frown a mark of his annoyance. Now that he walked closer, I spotted a different sort of badge or emblem near his nametag.

"*What*, Barbara?" he groused in the direction of our new neighbor.

"Are you just going to make those poor women freeze out there?" she sassed.

Losing his irksome scowl, he faced Ella and me. "Well, no. Ma'am, you can head inside. Sorry if you thought you needed to wait out here."

At that same moment, the officer I'd let into the house jogged down the back steps, shaking his head. "Not sure about that, either," he added.

"Whadaya mean, Donn?" Chief Mooney asked.

"No heat." Officer Donn shuddered, rubbing his arms. "Maybe old Fred didn't think to have the furnace checked out recently." Casting a polite smile of pity at me, he added, "Or you bought the place as is and didn't know?" The young man raised his brows in question.

"I didn't buy it. He left it to me." I exhaled harshly. "I checked last week that the utilities would be turned on before we came."

Officer Donn shook his head. "I fiddled with it and tried the thermostat on the wall, but nothing. As far as I can tell, gas and electric are hooked up. I just think the furnace died." His face froze as he glanced at the shed, likely realizing his slip of the tongue. "I mean, I think the furnace reached the end of its life."

"That's, like, saying the same thing," Ella deadpanned.

Officer Donn seemed to bite his tongue as he shrugged. "Yeah. Yes, it is. Just trying to be delicate in the circumstances and all…" His youthful baby face and apparent discomfort had me thinking he might be new to the force.

"Mooney, you can't expect them to stand out here all night!" Barbara shouted from next door.

A couple more men at the crime scene chuckled at her nagging hollers.

Mooney gritted his teeth. "Barbara, be quiet and mind your—"

"Are they suspects?" she insisted instead.

Mooney crossed his arms, facing her house to glare at her. "You don't even know what happened over here for them to be suspects of!"

"We found a body in the shed," Ella inserted.

I gently elbowed her. She gave me a wide-eyed stare of *so what?*

"Don't…shout about it to the whole world," I scolded.

"What kind of a body?" Barbara asked as she tilted her head to the side.

"What kind of body do you think?" Ella yelled back. "A dead one!"

"A person?" Barbara asked, lowering one arm to rest a spatula against her apron.

"It's not like a dead raccoon would need this many cops to come calling, would it?" Ella shouted back. "Yes, a person. Some woman."

I covered my face and clutched my daughter's sleeve. "Ella. It's a crime scene. They're investigating it and… You can't just broadcast this stuff to whoever's around!" Right? But then my call to 911 would be public information at some point. And this baking neighbor should have the right to know a corpse was near *her* property, too.

What a first impression we're making here.

"A woman?" Barbara asked. "Hmm. Who—"

"That's enough, Barbara," Mooney warned.

Barbara didn't seem bothered by the chief's tone or Ella's announcement of a murder so close to her home. "Well, are you two suspects?"

Bristling at the woman butting in, Mooney growled and rubbed a gloved hand over his face. "Barbara! Just go back inside and mind your own—"

"But, are we?" Ella asked him.

He frowned at her, then back at our neighbor, and sighed at me.

"Because, like we said, we weren't even here until this afternoon. And she looked deader than that," Ella insisted.

I reared back, frowning at her. "How would you know what a, well, a fresh…um…kill looks like?" *I can't believe we're even discussing this, let alone living through this!*

"Duh." She raised her brows at me. "*Mind Hunter.*" Then she gave the chief her *you can't have the last word* face, as though her watching that junk on TV made her an expert. "So we can't be suspects."

"No. Not officially," he admitted.

I slanted my brows at him gaping at his choice of words. "But we could be suspects *unofficially*?"

"No!" Mooney threw his hands up. "No, but like you said, this is an open investigation. It's too early to make any conclusions—"

"Do they have to stand around in the cold while you try to conclude something about this dead woman in the shed?" Barbara demanded.

"Barbara!" Mooney turned in her direction again. "Mind your own—"

"Oh, shut it. Don't forget I'm older than you. Bossing me around like that, telling me to mind my own business." She scoffed. "*My* business is looking out for my neighbors. And that means if I think you're being a slow, dull-headed idiot keeping them out in the cold for no good reason, I'll butt in as I please. Ladies," she said to us. "Would you like to warm up inside for a minute?" Propping her hip against the door, she pushed it further open.

Warm, bright light shone from what looked like a kitchen in the middle of a baking fest. As she permitted a better view into her home, the wind cut through again, now bringing with it the scents of nutmeg and cinnamon. I nearly smiled at the idea of thawing myself near a hot oven loaded with baked treats.

Ella nodded, already jogging that way.

"Ell!" I opened and closed my mouth, glancing at Mooney. Not for permission, per se, but well, he was the chief, and it looked like I was the new homeowner of a crime scene. It seemed prudent to check.

He smirked at Barbara still, and I tugged on his sleeve to get his attention. "Is there a reason we shouldn't go there to warm up for a while?"

His grunt wasn't a clear answer. The long-suffering sigh that followed didn't tell me much either. "No," he relented. "Go on. Go on. Just…don't take everything she says as fact."

We're moving in next to a chronic liar?

"My cousin likes to spout nonsense is all," he clarified. "Go ahead. Sorry if you assumed you had to wait outside."

Maybe work on your communication skills then, mister.

"I'll stop by as soon as I can," he promised with one more scowl at Barbara's house.

Chapter Three

I jogged after Ella, eager to feel something in my frozen fingers and toes again. As I made my way up the three steps to join her, Barbara's yell into her house came clearly and loudly. "Ingrid! We have company!"

The shout almost held the same nagging tone she'd used to chat with Chief Mooney outside. Perhaps this Ingrid was another relative? Oh, maybe her daughter. I bet that was it because I often summoned Ella in that same way. Tired, but not. Authoritative, but not.

From the distance, I pegged Barbara to be about sixty, but she was nimble and sassy, so what did I know? I felt confident she had to be older than me but not old enough to be my mother.

Ella was already at the front door, lingering in the small nook that Barbara's side door led to. Standing on one leg in that athletic grace and balance she did not inherit from me, Ella paused, removing her boot.

"What are you doing?" Barbara asked.

Ella raised one brow at her, stilling like a flamingo. "Taking…my boot off?"

Barbara only frowned, watching her intently.

I joined Ella in glancing around the nook that seemed to double as a small mudroom. Coats and purses—*is that a rain poncho with Dolly Parton?*—were hung on hooks. Scarves, mittens, and hats displayed a jumble of colors and patterns from inside a hemp-like basket. But no shoes waited on a tidy mat.

"Why?" Barbara asked bluntly, like Ella was being frivolous.

"Because…that's what people do?" my daughter said in a question, throwing Barbara's attitude back at her.

Barbara shrugged. "I don't."

"Other people do," Ella said.

Again, our neighbor shrugged.

"Ella." I wasn't sure what to add to my weak scolding, but didn't she ever *hear* how combative she sounded?

"Don't you know that, like, shoes bring a ton of germs into your home? Microbial pathogens and bacteria that can be carried on the soles?" Ella said, pointedly glancing at Barbara's hot pink sneakers.

I wanted to smack my face. She was accusing this gracious neighbor of being dirty? Could she not censor herself anymore?

"Oh, hey," another woman said as she walked down the hallway. Taller and thinner with paler features, she looked us over. "I heard we had company. Not a brainiac."

"It's true," Ella insisted, smushing her foot back into her boot.

"Good thing we mop often, then," Barbara quipped. She tipped her chin at the other woman's well-worn shoes. "Ingrid's flat-footed so she doesn't like to be barefoot or in slippers and sandals. Just the habit of the household."

I smiled and quickly thrust out my hand to shake. Realizing I still wore my glove, I pulled it back and removed the supposedly fleece-lined garment. "And what a lovely house it is. Thank you for offering us a break from the cold. I'm Naomi."

Barbara shook my hand but chuckled lightly. "Oh, we don't have to be so formal."

I winced. Did living for so long with Blane and his uppity family ruin me? The only way I could be personal was in a stuffy manner?

"I'm Barbara Caret." She squeezed my hand in an affectionate gesture before gesturing to the other woman."

She lifted a hand in a wave. "Ingrid. Ingrid Bosmer." I felt less embarrassed when she offered her hand, too. *See. It's a normal thing to do. Maybe Barbara is just…casual.*

"And this is Ella." I introduced my daughter, who seemed to peer around at the nook, taking in every detail of the unmatching décor and the fashion of the outerwear Barbara and Ingrid preferred.

"Hi," she said finally, almost smiling.

Barbara leaned in conspiratorially to me. "Will she be able to handle the shoe-transported microbial pathogens in the house?"

"I'm not a germaphobe," Ella insisted.

"Well, then come on in. No point standing at the door," Ingrid said as she walked by, gesturing with a crook of her finger to follow her.

I finished removing my coat, frowning at Ella as she trailed after Ingrid. Barbara held my garment, waiting for me to hand over my scarf and not-so-warm gloves. "Is she always like that?"

"She really isn't a germaphobe." I sighed, folding my scarf in half. "I think she's just used to it." Pointing at my boots, I said, "Used to taking them off at all her relatives' and friends' houses. Outrageous and immaculate mansions and such."

Barbara caught the snark in my statement and smiled. "Ah. I'm afraid to say we're much more laidback here in Fayette. Where are you moving from? I knew Fred was leaving his place to a relative, but he couldn't remember where you'd settled."

"Swenton."

Barbara's brows raised. "Fancy."

I smirked halfheartedly. "That's one way to put it."

We headed down the hall, the same way Ingrid had led Ella. "Is Ella always so…"

"Argumentative? Blunt? Yes. Is any teenager *not*?"

"Oh, boy." Barbara patted my back. "I was going to offer to start a new pot of English Lavender tea, but maybe you need a dash of bourbon instead."

Please? After the discovery at our new home, I didn't know if I'd turn that down. Once we'd found that woman in the shed, I'd snapped into a shell-shocked state of confusion, stunned at a corpse waiting for us when we were counting on a fresh new start in life.

Maybe a nice stiff drink would jerk me back into feeling something other than the numbed repetition of *what is going on?* racing in my mind.

Ella stood with Ingrid in the kitchen. Or perhaps *kitchen* wasn't the correct term. *Teacup collection site?* On a wooden shelf that ran along the walls, completing a complete perimeter, sat teacups. Commercial white ones with restaurant or café names. Dainty china with looping edges and whimsical paintings. Vividly colorful mismatching modernistic cups. Several mugs. And then the teapots. Those held real estate of their own, taking up a long yet narrow shelf above a stove.

"Wow," I mumbled to myself, my gaze dancing back and forth as I tried to take it all in.

"Are you a hoarder?" Ella asked Ingrid.

This time, I did smack my face. My patience was shot, and my nerves were frayed from the commotion of the body next door. "Ella. Just because your father's family is rude and judgy doesn't mean you can go around being a brat to everyone you meet."

"Eh," Ingrid said, dismissing her with a wave as she turned to the stove, sliding a kettle to a burner. "It was only a question."

I deadpanned at Ingrid's back. *Only a question.* If she heard those "questions" so often, she'd begin to wonder.

"Yeah, Mom." Ella lifted her hand at the drinkware lining the space. "That's *a lot* of teacups and teapots."

I shot her a stern look, praying she'd zip it. Now that we were in here, cozy near the warmth of the stove, I didn't want to go back outside and wait for Chief Mooney to bless us with news.

"Not enough though," Ingrid said cheerily. "I do collect them." She turned, setting her back to the stove and crossing her arms over her baggy green sweater. "It's a hobby of mine."

Barbara scoffed, pulling out a couple of chairs for Ella and me at the square table. "Hobby. More like an obsession."

Ingrid narrowed her eyes. "A *hobby*."

"To each their own!" I said, infusing a hopeful, bubbly lilt to my voice as I sat. Were these women sisters? Friends? Something else? It was no business of mine, but if they were the kind to bicker and rib each other, maybe I would be better off waiting outside in the cold. My head couldn't handle any more drama—jovial or not—for the night.

"Exactly," Ingrid said, taking a seat across from me.

Ella plopped into the chair to my right, and Barbara joined us after she brought a plate of almond-colored biscuits to us. "Fresh out of the oven." She smiled wide and wiggled her hips, setting into her seat. Her eyes lit up with excitement as she slid empty coffee mugs toward us.

Coffee mugs to use but teacups to decorate? Hmm.

"Now. Before the kettle calls. Spill the tea!"

Ingrid rolled her eyes. "What tea?"

Barbara huffed. "The dead woman they found next door! What else?"

"Like Mike Mooney was going to tell them anything," Ingrid argued.

"Of course not. He gets so secretive about 'cases' that I bet he'll hoard the scoop as long as he can. Make himself seem more important."

Ingrid lifted her hand in a *there you go* manner. "So, again, what tea? They won't have any details to share."

"Of course, they would," Barbara said as the kettle whistled. "They've got eyes. They found her."

Ingrid scoffed as she stood to tend to the tea.

"Well!" Barbara shimmied in her seat again. "Who was it?"

Ella laughed once. "Um. How would we know?"

I raised my hand to butt in. "We *just* moved here."

Barbara slanted her brows, looking at Ella and then me like we were missing a few marbles. "But *I'll* know. What'd she look like?"

"Ignore her," Ingrid said from the stove. "I bet you're trying to forget it all, not dwell on it."

Actually, yes. Thank you. That'd be nice. "It wasn't grisly," I said instead, unable to simply dismiss the image of the woman. More than anything, I couldn't merely wish away the fact a corpse had been waiting for me at my new residence.

"No blood? No weapons?" Ingrid asked, apparently ready to contradict her gentle suggestion *not* to talk about this. She sat, pouring steaming tea into our mugs. As she emptied the pot, Barbara bustled to the fridge, returning with milk, sugar, lemon, and—

"Is that maple syrup?" Ella asked, her nose scrunched.

"I'm too eager to hear the tea to make a real London Fog," she said, sliding the glass bottle to my daughter. "But if you have a sweet tooth, try it."

I stuck with lemon. I wasn't too big of a tea drinker. How could I be when Blane was such a coffee snob? The last time I made tea he'd griped about the "stench" and how the sink was "stained" that I almost wanted to find an air freshener just to mess with him. Goodness, he'd complained about any little thing… Like I was a fool to want something old-fashioned and simple like a cup of tea I made myself instead of using his extravagant and complicated espresso machine.

"No blood, no weapons." I sat up straighter. "Maybe she just…died. Something natural. A heart attack or stroke or…"

"Then why would she be in the shed, Mom?" Ella asked.

"Trespassing?" I guessed.

"*Who* was she, though?" Barbara glanced at the window that would show a view of our backyard if we cared to stand up and snoop at the Fayette cops investigating the scene. "What'd she look like? We were born and raised here. If you can describe her, we can identify her."

Ingrid smirked at Ella as she raised her teacup to her lips. "And don't say *dead*," she drawled.

What is this, a game of Guess Who? "She was shortish. Um, black hair," I said.

"What kind of hair?" Barbara pressed.

"Like an overgrown bob she forgot to have trimmed. Neglected highlights, too. Her blonde roots were showing," Ella said.

"Hmm." Barbara and Ingrid shared a pensive look. "What else?"

"What was she wearing?" Ingrid asked. "Glasses?"

"No. No glasses that I could tell. Um, black leggings with holes cut at the bottom, like crisscrosses for style. A white sweatshirt."

"A hoodie," Ella added.

"Slightly overweight but not overall," I said, frowning as I tried to picture the woman sprawled on the ground.

"Pear-shaped?" Barbara asked, patting her tummy.

"Kind of, yeah. Like she had a pooch, but her face was slimmer," I added. "I didn't look long, honestly."

"Just really pale skin. No makeup. Eyes staring up and not moving at all." Ella even made an expression, her tongue hanging down. "Mouth open."

I stared at her, worried not for the first time this night that she might have nightmares and horrors about what we'd found.

"Like season five or eight?" Ella said.

"Huh?" I squinted at her.

"*American Horror Story*, Mom!"

I rolled my eyes, hating how she liked watching that scary stuff. *Okay, I'm sure she'd be more traumatized from that than from that woman lying there in the shed.*

Then she slapped the table, almost startling me. "Oh! She wore dark-yellow and orange shoes. They stood out because they looked brand-new."

Ingrid sat up straighter, setting her mug down. "Any anklets?"

I nodded. What a specific thing to ask… "Yeah. These really tiny, thread-like gold chains. One had charms, some kind of ball or pendant. Then a corded one, too."

"Aha!" Ingrid exclaimed confidently.

Barbara nodded, a smug, knowing expression on her face. "Yasmin LeFleur. She's gotta be the body in your shed."

AUBREY ELLE

Chapter Four

They sure don't seem heartbroken…

Barbara and Ingrid didn't give the impression they were upset about this Yasmin LeFleur's death.

If it's her. They were only speculating based on our descriptions.

Then again, those flashy, gaudy shoes don't seem like something too many people would wear.

"Is she…was she a friend of yours?" I ventured to ask carefully.

"Nah." Ingrid waved a dismissive hand at us, the motion of the air sending the wafting steam above my mug to slip sideways as it rose. She sure made it hot!

"Not a friend, exactly," Barbara said.

"An acquaintance?" Ella asked.

Ingrid snorted at that. "Acquaintance? That'd be an understatement. She tried to not only be acquainted with everyone and everything happening in Fayette but also tried to proclaim herself all-knowing."

"A busybody?" I asked, hating how it felt like I was disrespecting the dead.

"Bingo," Barbara said.

"The police chief seemed to think you are a busybody, too," Ella told her, her brows raised as she raised her mug to sip her tea.

"Oooooh…" Ingrid teased, giggling and bobbing her hand. "I like her."

Barbara smirked at my daughter, and the good-natured ribbing had me fighting a smile.

"Ha. Ha," she said dryly. "I merely wanted to know why all of Fayette's officers happened to be next door."

"Hm-mmm," Ingrid said, implying she thought the opposite.

"Okay. Fine. I'm curious. I like to know who's doing what." Barbara shrugged and crossed her arms, as though that was her story and she was sticking to it. "I'll admit it. Unlike *you*." She narrowed her eyes at her friend.

Ingrid wisely shook her head. "Hey, I don't have to fess up to anything. I just…tag along for the ride. An indirect informant via your unquenchable nosiness."

"I'm not nosy like Yasmin, though!" Barbara sassed.

"No." Ingrid's teasing mood simmered as she frowned. "Being nosy is an expected trait of retirees in a small town. But Yasmin took it too far."

"How?" I asked. "Assuming that was who we found in the shed, of course."

"Yeah, what makes you so sure it's Yasmin?" Ella piped up.

"Those anklets." Barbara pointed at me. "You described them to a T."

"Were they special for some reason?" I asked. They hadn't struck me as unique. Certainly nothing expensive or rare. If she hadn't been wearing those leggings with the crisscross slits open at her ankles and low cut socks, I bet I never would have noticed so quickly.

"Those little pendant balls were bells," Ingrid said. "So her cats would always know when she was home and come running."

Ella and I said nothing, glancing at each other. Ingrid had said it with such a straight face, she couldn't have been making it up. Barbara seemed to hold back a laugh, though.

"Her cats, as in her pets?" I asked. "Not…a pied-piper-summoning-animals sort of thing?"

"Pied piper?" Barbara lost it then. "No. Nothing like that! Boy, you two must think you're traveling back to a primitive, medieval time by moving to a small place like Fayette!"

"Yes, her pet cats," Ingrid confirmed, nodding. "Yasmin practically devoted her life to those cats. If you ask me, those cats are what cost Yasmin her—"

The side door shut. Barbara had been giggling so much at my false guess that I hadn't noticed it'd be opened.

"Oh, for crying out loud," Chief Mooney said as he ambled down the hall toward us in the kitchen. "Barbara, I told you to mind your own business."

She sniffed, shaking her head like mocking his haughty tone.

"Need I remind you, this murder is a—"

"Murder?" I asked. Until now, I had been subconsciously clinging to the hope that woman had just happened to die. Out of coincidence, she just happened to be near that shed of all places and passed away from a natural cause. The alternative—accepting that a murder had happened at our new home—wasn't a rosy consideration.

Chief Mooney opened and closed his mouth before saying, "Yes. Murder."

"How?" Ella asked, glancing in the direction of our house. "How was she killed?"

Again, he did that guppy action with his mouth. I had to wonder how long he'd been in charge of law enforcement here. He sure seemed to hesitate with what to say, like he needed a few more practice runs of learning how to keep his mouth shut when he was stuck answering hard questions.

"Knife wound," the chief replied. "That's only a preliminary conclusion. The autopsy will provide more answers."

"Wow." I shared a look with Ella. Now that I couldn't hang on to the hope that it was an innocent death, I struggled to rationalize how safe our new home could be.

Chief Mooney must have noticed my unease because he was quick to add—for once, not hesitating with his words—a reassurance. "We have no reason to believe she was stabbed *there*, in Fred's, well, your shed."

"She was moved there? Dumped in the shed?" Ingrid asked.

"Yeah." Ella scoffed. "Like that's any better."

Barbara patted her hand on the table. "Fayette truly is a safe place, Ella. My cousin might be dull at times, and he might not be the most personable—like not thinking to tell you to wait somewhere warm while he investigated a crime scene—but he does his job well."

He deadpanned at her, his mouth an unmoving line of annoyance. "Thanks. Yeah, thanks."

"Are they allowed on the crime scene, then?" Ingrid asked.

"Instead of freezing outside while your crew investigates?" Barbara said.

He shook his head. "They can head on into the house."

I winced. "Without heat? I'd rather not." At Barbara's frown, I filled her in about the furnace being out.

"Oh, you can stay here. It's been a while since we've had someone in the guestroom," Ingrid said.

"Are you sure?" I asked. These ladies sure kept things entertaining, enough that they distracted me from the shock and worry of our discovery. Their easy camaraderie and welcome fooled me into looking too far into it. Such that they were, or would be, good friends. I'd been isolated with my ex and his toxic family for so long that I couldn't remember having a chat with a friend—not a relative, not a coworker, and not a parent of one of Ella's friends. A stranger who simply wanted to spend time with me without an ulterior motive.

It's pity, Naomi. They pity you and feel sorry about it all.

I hoped that wasn't it.

"Of course, we're sure." Barbara stood quickly. "I love playing hostess."

"Yeah, right," Chief Mooney drawled. "You just love having the inside scoop, and with them just moving into town, you want to get all the gossip first."

"Jealous of her fact-finding skills?" Ella teased.

I choked on a laugh. The audacity of this brat. Talking like that to a police chief, of all people!

He took it in stride, though, almost smiling at her but ending up rolling his eyes. "Facts? Gossip. That's all it is."

"But it *was* Yasmin," Barbara said as she breezed down the hall, excited to prepare the guestroom. "That's a fact I uncovered without your help."

He groaned. "Please, just… Don't stay up all night making assumptions and feeding rumors into their heads. You know how news—true or not—spreads in town."

"Yeah, yeah," Ingrid said. "We know. We know. But that's the difference between us—I mean, Barbara—and Yasmin. We're not going to stand on the roof and announce anything about this. We know how to keep a secret."

He wagged a finger at her. "See that you do. At least until it is shared publicly." Facing me, he sighed, relaxing his shoulders as he dropped his teasing with them and peered at me more professionally. "You'll stay here then?"

I narrowed my eyes, standing to help Ingrid gather our mess from the tea. "Are you asking because my whereabouts matter in the case?"

"Not exactly." He shrugged. "You're not a suspect, Ms. Front."

I resisted a wince. I had to follow through and change my name sooner than later. Every time I heard it, it was a step backward.

"We've already confirmed your alibi."

I jerked, nearly dropping the mugs in my hands. "My alibi?"

"Yes. You and your daughter weren't in Fayette at the estimated time of death."

I swallowed. *Oh, no.* "How did you confirm that?"

He frowned at me slightly. "I called the manager of the hotel you said you'd been staying at for the last couple of weeks."

I groaned, wanting to bury my face in my hands. I would have if they'd been empty.

"What?" Ingrid asked, gently taking the mugs from me.

Ella brought the plate of biscuits to the counter. "That means the manager will have told my dad that something bad has happened here. Dad knows everyone in Swenton. And now he'll give her a hard time about it."

Just what I don't need. Steve giving me another headache about Ella's custody. The minute he learned a dead body was waiting for us at our new home… I'd never hear the end of it!

Ella bumped her shoulder into mine. "And he'll just have to get over it. It's not like we're in danger here, are we?" she asked the chief.

"*Here?*" Ingrid asked, pointing down to emphasize we were talking about her house now. "You're as safe as you can be here."

But what about next door?

"Again, I can't provide too many details as the investigation continues. I'll have a patrol drive by—not only as a precaution to the residents on this street but also to make sure no one tries to snoop around the crime scene."

I nodded.

"I agree with Ingrid," he said.

"Hurry, write that down," she said in a stage whisper to Ella.

The chief smirked at her before facing me again. "Given the suspected time of Ms. LeFleur's death, I don't think you or your daughter are in any immediate danger here, Ms. Front."

"Because she was killed a while ago?" I asked.

"The coroner gave us a preliminary date of death of about three days ago," he replied.

That did make me feel marginally better. Maybe it was a one-and-done and the killer moved on. A fluke.

"I would, however, like to make sure my crew has access to the area," Chief Mooney said. "And if we have any questions, to know where we can reach you."

I glanced at Ingrid, who smiled warmly. "If you're sure…"

"Positive. And I've got a number for someone who could help with that furnace."

The black cat clock on the wall swished her tail and roved her eyes side to side as she let me know it was already almost eight. Ella kept late hours whereas insomnia kept me up at all hours. "Probably too late to call them now." *And a late call at an emergency rate would be so much more expensive.* I almost shook myself, chiding myself for worrying about such a trivial thing like an HVAC repair. Or replacement. Someone had been murdered nearby, yet as alarming as that concept was as a principle, I wasn't too worried—not if the police chief wasn't.

"Likely. You and Ella are more than welcome to stay the night. More than that if the furnace looks like a longer project."

Now I did shake my head. "I sure hope not."

Chief Mooney rapped his hand on the hallway's doorframe, heading back to the side door. "I'm a phone call away, ladies. And *please.* Please don't be feeding nonsense into your guests, Ingrid. I'd say it's bad enough that she had to be welcomed to town with a body in the shed, but she doesn't need a coming attraction report of all the bad gossip."

Ingrid gave him her back to roll her eyes at me. Then she saw him outside.

"Are we interrupting?" I rushed to ask, now that my senses were returning somewhat. I appreciated

Ingrid and Barbara offering us a place to lodge for tonight, but it seemed like such a generous and overwhelming offer from people we'd only just met. Ella and I couldn't barge in here and impose.

"Oh, not at all." As she walked back to me, she studied me closely. "Honestly, don't worry. We're just two best friends. Retired, bored, and maybe too curious for our own good."

"We're not ruining any plans?"

Ingrid smiled wide, her green eyes twinkling. "Just a viewing of *Jeopardy*, but I'm sure Ella would have us beat and ruin the fun."

I laughed, joining her after she tipped her head to the side, suggesting we go find Barbara.

Upstairs, I felt deceived by how spacious their home was. It was an ordinary two-story brick house, just like the one I inherited next door, but the interior held more room than I thought it would. Four bedrooms, two on each side of a hallway, with two full bathrooms at the ends. Downstairs, I'd caught a glimpse of at least one more bedroom that they seemed to have converted into a library. Shelves upon shelves of books hid in the shadows of that room. I'd almost slowed down just to get a better peek, feeling like Belle in the Beast's castle.

Blane had a "library" in the mansion he wanted to call our home. But most of the tomes were fakes—stand-ins to look impressive for guests. The books I loved and devoured were relegated to piles in my tiny office, shoved aside and never to be seen. More than once I'd found the housekeeper stashing them in the closet, just so no one would have to—as my mother-in-law had worded it—"realize I read trash for simple-minded women."

I rolled my eyes, annoyed again by another memory of him popping up.

"Ella, you pick first," I said in the biggest guestroom that Barbara had prepared.

She looked between the two double beds, seeming to compare the two. Then she glanced at the window, which happened to be on a wall that faced our house next door.

"That one." Her finger was aimed at the bed further from the wall. Furthest from our new house.

After a few more promises that we weren't intruding on their evening, and that they wouldn't be put out in the morning, Ingrid and Barbara left us to settle in for the night. Ella plopped on the bed she'd chosen, sighed in contentment at the plushness of the mattress, and pulled her phone out.

"You're not going to post about what we found, right?" She was months from eighteen, a true adult according to the law. Yet I couldn't resist the instinct to drill in the need for confidentiality.

"Why would I say anything about that?" She shook her head, not even making eye contact. "It's not like it's something to brag about. I'm not proud of the fact that dump had a dead body in it."

"It wasn't *in* the house, though."

She shot me a blunt look. "Really? That's the silver lining you're going to stick to? That we're 'lucky' Yasmin LeFleur wasn't in the house?"

I shrugged, checking out the posters on the wall. The Beatles. Jimi Hendrix. The Who. CCR. Even the Beach Boys. "Well, I'm glad she wasn't in the house." It would've made it much harder to want to go in and live there."

"We still *haven't* gone in there."

And tonight, we were staying at a neighbor's, a pair of friends who were practically strangers. People Blane had never met and vetted and would likely not approve of simply because they weren't in his circle of wealthy friends.

"Hopefully the furnace guy they know will work fast, then." I left her with that comment, not in the mood to hear her whining. I'd told the gals I wanted to retrieve our duffel bags of necessities from the truck, and Ingrid said she'd be downstairs watching TV, that she'd see me out and back in. What surprised me was that both Barbara and Ingrid sat in the living room, this space cluttered with so many houseplants I wondered if one of them used to be a horticulturist. Barbara was listening to an audiobook while Ingrid scowled at a crossword puzzle. When she spotted me, she grabbed the coat she had lying next to her on the couch. "I'll be your lookout."

I stilled, pausing to put my arm through my coat sleeve. "I thought the chief said it would be safe— relatively safe here."

"What?" Barbara yelled, squinting.

"Nothing," Ingrid shouted.

"Much fun?" Barbara asked louder. "What's much fun?"

"Oh, for Pete's sake,' Ingrid mumbled, ushering me outside with her. I couldn't help but laugh.

"You two have been friends for a while, huh?" I asked as I walked with her toward the rental truck.

"Since kindergarten," she replied, looking around at the yards cast in shadows of the cold winter night.

I hurried, both because I was cold and because the duffels were right where I expected them, tucked between our seats. After I grabbed them, I locked up and walked back to the house. Ingrid insisted on carrying one after I struggled with Ella's bulky bag.

"I swear, if I tell her to pack light, she hears it as reverse psychology," I joked.

"I'd say you both packed heavy," she teased, tilting her head at the truck we left behind us. "Packed it *all*."

I glanced at the house we were supposed to be moving all our things into. Dark, lonely, and that huge tree still swaying its branches every which way in the wind.

And who knows when—if—we'll be unpacking it there any time soon.

Despite the chief's estimation that we were safe in this neighborhood, I couldn't help but worry our arrival was a bad omen for a "fresh new start" in life.

AUBREY ELLE

Chapter Five

Ella showed no signs of a nightmare that night. Maybe it was the long drive that tired her out. Or the stress from finding a dead body. Then again, she was a mostly temperamental teenager prone to mood swings and hormones wreaking havoc on her. She usually enjoyed enviable deep, solid sleep.

Just wait 'til you're older, girlie. Just *wait. Relish this ease of falling asleep while you can.*

I sighed, nestling my head against the soft pillow. It was a shame I couldn't fall asleep already because this bed was probably one of the most comfortable places I'd ever rested. Firm but plush mattress, the softest sheets on earth, a perfect pillow.

Wind cracked a branch against the house, and I flinched.

No matter how cozy this bedroom was and how comfortable I could get in this bed, there was no escaping the sounds of an unfamiliar place.

And knowing a dead body had been next door.

I huffed out a breath and frowned at the ceiling. There was nothing for it. I wasn't sleeping anytime soon. May as well tire and dry out my eyes reading nonsense on my phone. I grabbed it from the nightstand between my bed and Ella's. After checking on the home screen that it was dimmed as much as possible, the device in night mode, I unlocked it.

Ella wasn't addicted to social media like her peers were back in Swenton. For that, I was grateful. I liked to think she was too smart for it, the pull of scrolling at nothing special not impacting her. I cared for it even less than she did. So much bullying, too many people pretending to be experts about everything and anything, and all the soliciting and ad-like posts people flooded the internet with. Worst of all, anything said would be fodder for Blane's relatives and friends to pick apart one hundred different ways.

Like this, for example. Another fundraising call for someone's life goals, or a pet adoption charity, or something of the like. Maybe I could start a PleaseFundMe for the furnace. Or the funds to hire someone to cut down that tree shedding in the front yard. *Not.* While being married to Blane—trying and failing to get used to his affluence—I was an old-fashioned girl at heart. I needed something, I'd work for it.

I rolled my eyes, scrolling past the junk and then tapping on the Fayette page. No, I wasn't going to beg for money. But I'd feel less miserable if I had a job to look forward to.

May as well make this insomnia work me for. No time like the present to get a feel for the wanted posts for Fayette. Skimming the recent posts citizens of Fayette had shared, I almost did a double-take, seeing that fundraising program again. Someone needing assistance and donations for…yada, yada, yada. Wait, what? Some Mark guy wanted donations just because he quit his job? A job he'd quit because his boss named Jameson wasn't okay with him not showing up on time all week? This guy didn't want to *join the masses of gullible sheep forfeiting their lives just to earn a paycheck* and had the audacity to ask for *donations* for an easy life? In the picture with the post, Mark had his arm around a teen who looked no older than Ella. Asking for ten grand…because he was lazy? Sheesh. *How many of these are scams, anyway?*

On I went, seeing nothing like a call for help or *now hiring.* I sighed deeply. *It's early yet. We've got enough to get by for a while, but sooner or later…* Something had to pop up. And it would. I was sure of it.

My eyes weren't tired, though, so on I scrolled. Another fundraiser. Bake sale. Form to volunteer for the formal dance around Valentine's Day. I winced. Oh, boy. Ella *loathed* those events, but maybe it wouldn't feel like an obligation now, a competition with her peers, since she'd be the new student. I bet she'd see that as an excuse to not have to go, and I'd stand by her choice.

In Swenton, Ella's classmates had been so catty, so crazed about their formal dances like it was a defining moment of the rest of their lives.

Ha. Newsflash, it's not.

As I absently drifted further from the real worry of obtaining a job, I familiarized myself with the place I'd now call home. These smiling faces in pictures would be my fellow citizens, neighbors, and acquaintances.

I paused my thumb, hovering it over the screen as Ingrid's words came back to me.

"She tried to not only be acquainted with everyone and everything happening in Fayette but also tried to proclaim herself all-knowing."

Like a switch, I was even more awake. My worries about money and a job were no joke, but as a deep curiosity about the deceased hit me full-force, I wondered if I'd latched on to the tangible, normal concerns of a single mom as a subconscious way of distracting myself. Fretting about *my* woes as a way to avoid stressing about the even bigger, more pressing one of Yasmin LeFleur dead on my property.

I typed in a search for her name, and I wasn't disappointed. Numerous posts showed, and just as many comments replying to others. She sure had tried to butt into everyone's business online. Neighborhood watches, complaints about dog poop. If the garbage men could be quieted in the morning so as not to disturb her cats' sleeping.

I rolled my eyes. *I thought cats slept all day, anyway?* Then whining about the same garbage men "having the nerve" to want a Monday off after a holiday observed on a Sunday.

Wow.

I wasn't getting a rosy impression, and she was still a stranger to me in a large sense. From her social media presence alone, she came off as nosy, quick to complain, and even quicker to tattle-tale on anyone she crossed paths with.

On and on I scrolled, trying to get a feeling of who Yasmin LeFleur could have been other than the town's worst busybody. I was a firm believer that *every*one had something good about them. Not everyone could be *all* bad. Flaws could sometimes trump the goodness in a person, but it was human nature to have a little decency hiding underneath.

I couldn't find much to suggest a hint of Yasmin's decency, although I did agree with her sharing a post about the environmental hazards of things that weren't actually recyclable. She'd worded it in the vein of a complaint, concerned about her cats again, but I was in favor of a cleaner, more responsible world too.

The further back her posts were dated, I did a double-take at the name connected to her ID photo. A black-and-white noir type of portrait. The serious, looking-away kind of pose worked really well for some, but if anyone were to ask me for an opinion of Yasmin's choice of an ID thumbnail, I'd say it looked more like a mugshot than an artistic statement. What captured my attention, though, was the change. In the recent posts, she was Yasmin LeFleur, but a few in the middle only showed Yasmin G. No last name. *Strange.* Then even more dated posts showed Yasmin LeFleur again. Maybe it was a phase of trying to be mysterious, using an initial for ambiguity.

As I read on, I did achieve my initial goal of tiring out my eyes. I must have dozed off to a choppy yet dreamless sleep at some point because I jerked awake at a loud bang downstairs.

Heart racing, I bolted upright. Ella slept away in her bed.

It was faint, but I heard a gasp from downstairs.

Chapter Six

I came down to the kitchen and nearly gasped myself.

"That's…that's a lot of sugar," I commented.

Ingrid held a really neat ceramic container with a depiction of an idyllic garden painted on it. As she turned, facing me, I was intrigued by how, as she spun, the vase-like item showed a twist in the artwork as it morphed into an *Alice in Wonderland* kind of theme. Not psychedelic, or alluding to a hallucinogen, but so detailed it seemed to pull me in.

At her shoes—cloglike slippers with a solid sole— lay at least an inch of sugar.

She pushed her lips to one side in a tired pout. Resigned, she glanced at the sugar and then back at me, tucking the sugar pot between her arm and her side. "Sorry. Did I wake you?"

I yawned. "Yes and no. I'm not a great sleeper."

She pointed at me, nodding. "I'll make you some of my Roman Chamomile tea tonight. I've suffered from insomnia since my days in the military. It's the only thing that kind of helps to relax me enough that I ignore my tinnitus."

"Gosh. I'm sorry."

She set the sugar container on the table, gingerly stepping through the mess she'd made. When Ella and I came in through the side door last night, I noticed a small cut-in space where a hanging rack of cleaning supplies was stored. I retrieved two brooms and a dustpan.

"Sorry about what?" She took one broom from me and we began sweeping it up. "That I dropped a couple of weeks' worth of sugar on the floor?"

I paused, peering at her. "You'd consume this much sugar in two weeks?"

"Ha." She smiled, sweeping away. "You'd be surprised how much sugar is hidden in food as it is."

I nodded.

"Little thing like you, you probably don't have to worry about that much."

"More like stress is the ultimate appetite killer."

"Hmmm."

I loaded up the dustpan, and she brought over the garbage can.

"What were you sorry about, then?" she asked.

Shrugging, I emptied my pan. "About the tinnitus. Is it bad?"

"Oh, I've gotten used to it, but it's worse if I have a cold. Worse yet when rain is coming. I only notice it at night when I try to sleep. In the daytime, Barbara makes enough noise and talks so much I don't have a chance to hear it."

I smiled.

"And when she wakes up and realizes she won't be able to make you and Ella her favorite cinnamon buns for breakfast because I dumped the sugar, I'll never hear the end of *that*."

"Oh, she doesn't have to go through the trouble." But, wow. Now that she'd mentioned it, I wondered if they'd taste as good and unique as those tea biscuits we had last night.

"She enjoys it," Ingrid said, standing straight and frowning out the window instead of resuming her sweeping effort like me. "One of these days, I bet she'll get her way and talk me into opening a bakery and café."

"That'd be a lovely idea," I said. "Caffeine and sweets. My two favorite vices."

When I'm not so stressed about life that I allow myself to enjoy vices...

"But it sounds like *work*," she said. "And I'm not done enjoying retirement to go back to a job."

"Maybe if you love it, it won't seem like work?"

She did that one-sided smirk again, like silently replying *maybe, maybe not.* I frowned, wondering why she wasn't sweeping. I didn't mind stepping in and offering a helping hand. Before my mother passed away, that was precisely how she'd raised me—to never shy from assisting others.

"You okay?" I asked as she tore her gaze from the window to the artistic container on the table. She was so pensive, I wasn't sure if she'd heard me, but I didn't want to break the early-morning silence again.

"I lost my grip on the sugar container because I could have sworn I saw someone running through there," she said, pointing at the window.

I gasped.

Her finger indicated the window that would show a view of the parallel driveways between our houses. A view of the shed!

"See?" She raised her brows at me. "You gasped too."

I leaned the broom against the table to approach the window. "You saw someone?"

"I thought I did. I hadn't turned the lights on yet, but I could have sworn I saw something dart by." She joined me in peering out the window, our breaths fogging on the cold glass. I wrapped my robe around myself, tugging the belt to a tighter knot.

"Someone messing with the crime scene?" I asked as I looked toward the shed. The doors were shut now, and earlier, I'd noticed the techs loading her body up to take away. Nothing looked amiss. Just the old, raggedy shed. My attention was pulled from the ordinary—if ancient—shed. Blue, yellow, then magenta lights flashed in the distance, the glare of a TV from the neighbor's window on the other side of my house.

"Who knows?" Ingrid said as she backed up. "Who knows if I even saw something? Might have just been a play of light from Mrs. West's TV." She'd said the last part in a drawl of annoyance. "She *never* shuts it off."

"Maybe she should invest in a timer," I said as we resumed sweeping the sugar. Once we were done, the chore no problem with the easy quiet between us, Ingrid offered to make a pot of Earl Grey. A good cure to chase away the morning sluggishness and promote smart thinking, something she deemed we'd need with such a mystery between our houses.

"Unless you'd prefer to go back to bed," she added as she set the kettle to boil. "Barbara likes to sleep in when she stays up all night reading." She snorted. "And I don't think I heard her go up to her bedroom until well after one. If she gets hooked on a good book, she'll stay up all night sometimes."

I took a seat at the kitchen table. Running my finger along a groove in the wood, I sighed. "No, thanks. It's a useless feat. I'm up, and I'd love a cup of your Earl Grey." Since I had her attention and I didn't have to worry about an interruption this early in the morning—I assumed—I asked her about Yasmin.

"What were you going to say last night, when Chief Mooney stopped in before he left?"

Ingrid partly turned, one brow raised in question.

"You said you thought Yasmin's cats cost her something." I lifted my phone from my robe pocket and set it on the table. I'd grabbed it when I heard her gasp, fearing I'd need to call 911. Finding that dead body sure had me hyperaware of emergencies striking from nowhere. I had a hunch we were all on edge, like the seemingly formidable Ingrid dropping a sugar container from surprise.

Shaking my phone slightly, I said, "When I couldn't sleep, I tried to tire my eyes out reading about who she was."

Ingrid nodded. "And boy, she sure liked to be known on social media." She carried two mugs to the table and sat, glancing back at the kettle once. "I thought Yasmin's cats cost her marriage, cost her Jasper, her ex-husband."

My brows shot up. Blane and I argued about so many things, petty and not, but a pet? There had never been wiggle room. He hated the idea of an animal going to the bathroom in his house or his yard. Having a pet was never up for discussion, and in the vein of trying to learn what battles to fight, I'd let it go.

"He had a yipping dog when they met. Or a couple. I don't remember. He might have had one terrier thing and then got the chihuahua after they married. *She* was firmly a cat person. Three of them, at least."

"And their contradicting preference for pets caused them to divorce?" I asked.

"It didn't sound like a happy situation," Ingrid said. "Constantly arguing about them in public. And you've got Ella, so maybe it won't resonate with you. Maybe you can't relate to the idea personally, but Yasmin treated those felines as though they were children. And Jasper considered his dogs as though they were his sons."

I nodded. "I can see it. Adopting a pet is like adopting something into your family."

"So considering it that way, from what they often argued about and what I heard, it would have been more like a case of their offspring not getting along. As much as they valued and cherished their pets..." She shrugged. "It was definitely grounds for conflict in what was probably already a poor match for marriage."

At the kettle's whistle, Ingrid got up. She set the water in and while the tea was steeping, she brought the pot to the table.

"What about you?" she asked as she sat again. "You mentioned an ex last night."

Her probing question was expected. I had told them I was divorced last night, and Ella sure hadn't refrained from suggesting he disliked me. Yet I wasn't bothered. Ingrid's gentle and matter-of-fact attitude made it seem more like a friend was simply checking on me, not a local busybody eager to know the latest gossip.

"I did. He's back in Swenton," I said.

"And did cats and dogs break that marriage up?"

I laughed, rolling my eyes at her as she poured my tea. "If only it could have been that simple. He disliked pets, so no. We didn't have that brand of disagreement. He cheated. I doubted he'd ever loved me. And I finally came to my senses, reading—" I paused, looking back at the hallway in case Ella had woken and could be eavesdropping, I sighed.

"Reading Ella's persuasive argument essay that she'd left out before the assignment was due. Where she argued against women carrying on old-school stereotypical traditions, like marrying straight out of high school because they were expecting a baby"—I pointed at myself—"because it isn't fair to the child to be raised in a loveless home."

Ingrid whistled.

"It forced me to stop making excuses and really dig in and look at it from her perspective. While we don't have his family's money, we're also now free of their expectations. And while we don't have luxuries and a huge mansion to call home, we have…" I winced as I trailed off, glancing at the window that faced our new house. "Well, we have a new start."

"No matter how rocky its beginning," Ingrid sat, patting my hand. "Barbara and I will be here to help you gals get that fresh start."

"Thank you, Ingrid. That means a lot." I'd received more grace and sympathy from her than I had from so-called friends and family in years.

"He didn't want custody?" she asked.

"Oh, he did. Does. It's a 'disgrace' for his child to be raised somewhere else. But she was firm in the family court. She's almost seventeen, so it's not long until she doesn't fall under custodial arrangements. Ella was clear that she didn't want to live with him or his new mistress, but I can't say the same about her enthusiasm to move *here*." I pressed my finger to the table in emphasis. "Even before we found Yasmin in the shed, she wasn't too happy about relocating to a small town in the middle of nowhere."

Ingrid smiled. "Oh," she said sagely before taking a sip of tea. "She'll come around."

Despite her cheery optimism, I slumped, my elbow on the table and my chin in hand. "Probably. But I don't want to know how Blane will react. He'll have plenty to say about a dead body at our new home, a home he was harshly critical of in the first place."

As though we spoke of the devil and summoned him, my phone rang.

Blane Front showed on the caller ID.

Defeated at the idea of having to speak to my ex this early in the morning, I lowered my head to rest on my forearm and groaned.

Chapter Seven

Barbara cracked a long, almost yodeling yawn as she entered the kitchen.

I lifted my head to say good morning to her before I summoned the guts—*not the desire*—to answer Blane's call.

She skidded, frowning at the floor. "Is that sugar?" she asked. My phone buzzed again as I stalled, and she cocked her head to the side. "And what was that *woe is me* groan?" she asked.

Ingrid sipped her tea and pointed at the phone. "Her good-for-nothing ex is calling." She scoffed. "I doubt he's waiting to wish her a good morning."

I had been careful *not* to talk bad about him, but she'd read between the lines anyway, summing him up as good-for-nothing independently.

"Oh." Barbara sniffed and looked at me. "Do you want to talk to him right now?"

"No. But I should an—"

Barbara picked up the phone, accepted the call, then hung up. She set the device on the table and nodded at me. "He can wait."

I gaped at her.

The phone buzzed again.

She grabbed it and answered, "She doesn't want to talk to you right now. Try later." Then she hung it up and set it down once more. Her tone held enough gravelly authority that Blane likely felt too intimidated to call again.

"Feel free to tell her if she's crossing a line," Ingrid said as she stood and stretched. "She'll never know otherwise."

"Well." Barbara set a hand on her hips and frowned at me. "*Did* you want to talk to him right now?"

I shook my head. "No. Thank you." I stood too, stretching before I leaned over to hug her. "You're an angel." I wasn't one to cower from Blane or his slightly harassing calls. I'd plunged myself into the entire divorce ordeal with a firm self-promise to stay levelheaded and not let him get to me—or push me over. Which should have been the first clue that Blane and I never matched. We'd argued often, but without emotion. Clinically, like we were strangers and not vested in what the other truly wanted. But having someone else share that sentiment with him for once was a relief. A woman needed a break sometimes.

"An angel?" Ingrid hooted a laugh as she went to the fridge. "That'll go straight to her big head. I dropped the sugar, though. Want eggs and toast instead of those cinnamon buns?"

Barbara scrunched up her face as she got a mug for herself. "*All* of the sugar?"

While Ingrid got busy with the bread and eggs, Ella staggered into the kitchen with all her morning glory. Scowling and eyes half-opened, she slumped into the seat Ingrid had vacated. "No coffee?" she whined.

I sighed, reminded of one of the many regrets with her. I tried my best, but I doubted I'd win mom of the year with Ella. Her forming a coffee habit before adulthood bugged me like nothing else.

"Meh. Who needs coffee?" Barbara said, pouring herself tea.

Ella shot her hand in the air, huffing. "Uh, me."

"You do not." Barbara seemed impervious to my teen's look of dismay. She slid another mug of Earl Grey her way. "Tea has caffeine too, you know. Especially black teas like this."

"Not enough."

"Maybe you just haven't had *good* tea," Ingrid inserted from the counter. "Not strong enough."

I cleared my throat, cutting off whatever retort Ella was brewing in her strong-minded will. "It's good, El." *For God's sake, don't show these sweet women how nasty you can be in the morning.*

She mumbled to herself, rubbing her face as she took the tea. "No syrup?"

Barbara mocked a gag. "Not with." Then she pursed her lips, peering at the sugar pot on the table. "At least we got enough in here."

While Ingrid began breakfast, I filled in Ella and Barbara about why there was such a sugar shortage this morning. Barbara didn't seem worried or alarmed about her housemate potentially spotting someone running between our yards. She confirmed it.

"It was Roxanna," she said before sipping her tea, docile as can be.

Ella perked up. "The woman heading up that pet portrait thing?"

I did a double-take at my daughter. When had she learned about pending businesses in our new town? She raised her brows at me, like prompting me to ask. "What? When you first said we were moving here, I took it upon myself to research a little."

Portrait. Now it clicked. I thought back to Yasmin's not-so-art noir image she'd chosen for her ID online. A few other posts shared a similar theme—

only with pets, not people. "Oh, that photo business…"

"Roxana and Yasmin had the idea to go into this little animal photography gig. As partners. Roxana used to dabble with art, offering adjunct photography and design classes at the community college. Yasmin…"

"She *thought* she was a photog genius," Ingrid supplied, seeming to fill in what Barbara had paused at—what Yasmin brought to the table in this business venture.

"Or she was the animal 'expert' of some kind," Barbara said. "Thought she was, at least."

Ella seemed to perk up more as we chatted. If it wasn't the tea waking her up, the gossip seemed to do the trick. "But it looks like the Roxana lady kicked Yasmin out of their efforts." She yawned, and when she was done, sitting upright more, she added, "The business page no longer lists Yasmin as admin. I looked last night while Mom got our duffel bags from the truck. I realized I'd heard of Yasmin before because I browsed at the pet photography service."

I had to chuckle. "Why? We didn't—don't have a pet."

"Doesn't mean I don't want one."

I picked up my phone, another smidgen of guilt hitting me for depriving Ella of a pet all her life. She wouldn't have to work hard to sway me. If searched online again and saw the posts of dogs, cats, and even bunnies Roxana had begun to share, spreading the word about her upcoming grand opening of services. *Too cute.*

"It looks like Roxana started the business page with Yasmin but then removed her."

"Because they had a falling out," Barbara said. "Some argument or something other. Yasmin thought Roxana was taking over. Too bossy. Which seemed to bother her because she felt her ideas would ruin the business's hope for success."

"And I hear Roxana was bitter about being the only one making all the investments," Ingrid said at the stove, eggs already in the pan. She asked for our egg preferences, and I was relieved Ella wasn't going to be picky and make the kind woman go to further trouble. "I was in line at the post office, oh, maybe a couple of months ago. Around Halloween at least," Ingrid continued. "She was ranting and fussing, making a big deal about some postal insurance that backfired. It sounded like she'd ordered background sheets—"

"Backdrop," Ella interrupted.

"Uh-huh. You knew what I meant," Ingrid said. "She'd ordered holiday *backdrops*, but they were damaged in shipping, and she thought Yasmin had chosen the delivery insurance but she hadn't."

"Stuff like that," Barbara said. "They sure didn't seem like compatible business partners."

"And that was who was running between our yards this morning?" Ingrid asked.

Barbara nodding. "I'd just left the bathroom, walking back to my room to figure out my outfit for later."

"And decided to go with imitating the sun?" Ella quipped.

I smiled, giggling at Barbara's attire. A sequined yellow skirt above white leggings, a golden tube top beneath an unbuttoned buttery cardigan, and a ruffly yellow-orange headband polka-dotted with red hearts. She was quite the image of sunshine.

"You like?" she asked, turning her shoulders one way and then the next.

"For a sixties costume?" Ella teased.

"Most of this *is* from the sixties," Barbara said with a wink. "I felt like we needed some brightness after yesterday. Anyway, as I walked by, something caught my eye. I figured it was Mrs. West's TV, as usual, but when I paused and looked down, I saw Roxana glancing back toward the shed."

"Maybe she was just curious." Ella jerked a thumb to indicate the front of the house. "Because when I came downstairs, I saw out the front door window a few walkers and runners slowing down to gawk at the house."

Ingrid brought a plate of toast over. I stood, going to the counter to grab the jellies and butter she'd set out, eager to help and not just be served here.

"Yasmin's death is big news," Barbara said. "It's not like we get too much excitement in a small town like Fayette."

I sat again, waiting for Ella and Barbara to take a slice before I did. "Which means everyone will be nosy and snooping at our new home. So much for a peaceful start."

"Oh, it'll fade. Unless there's a reason the location matters much, people will stop gawking," Barbara said.

"But I doubt people will stop talking and wondering who did it," Ingrid countered as she brought the scrambled eggs to the table.

"We haven't even set foot in the house yet," I said.

"I'm not sure I want to now," Ella said between bites.

"It's all we've got for now, Ella," I reminded her gently. No shame warmed my cheeks at admitting that in front of Ingrid and Barbara. I was sure they could infer that I had no other place to go after my divorce from what I'd told them this far. More than that, I felt confident they weren't the kind to judge and ridicule it.

"And what's the problem with living next door, anyway?" Ingrid asked.

Ella deadpanned at her. "Gee, I don't know. A corpse."

"It wasn't *in* the house," I said.

"Close enough!" Ella sassed back. "I'm never going to want to even go near that shed now."

Barbara laughed once. Then just tear it down. Throw some grass seed down and you'd never know it was even there."

"Then where will they store their tools and mower and such?" Ingrid asked.

Barbara brightened as though her friend's logical question was a light-bulb moment. "Seriously! Tear it down. It's an eyesore, no offense. Fred neglected it as he got older and never cared because he hired out the lawn care. Then build another shed—we'll pitch in for it. Just build it at the *other* corner of the yard. That way, it'll block the glare from Mrs. West's TV all night!"

I shrugged. Where the shed stood didn't really matter to me. "Maybe after the furnace is fixed," I said. One thing at a time. "I should head over there and at least check it out. Get an idea of what could be wrong."

"Because you know so much about heating appliances," Ella quipped.

I narrowed my eyes at her.

"I know someone who can help," Ingrid reminded me.

Finished with her eggs, Barbara wiped her mouth. "How about this, ladies? Since you two seem to think old Fred's house is going to have ghosts by association just because someone dumped Yasmin's body in the shed, I'll come with. Huh? Does that sound good?"

I couldn't put my finger on *why*, but it did. Barbara was a ray of brightness, and her flippant, down-to-earth calm was something I enjoyed. "Actually, I'd appreciate that."

She stood, collecting her things to carry to the sink. "Besides, Ingrid and I moved in here, what, fifteen years ago?"

"Seventeen," Ingrid said.

"I should remember most of what Fred had done to the house. I can give you a little tour of it all."

"Don't forget to mention when the basement flooded and he had all that waterproofing done," Ingrid said, raising her finger. "He had to have paid a pretty penny for it. A solid investment."

I nodded, gathering my things and feeling more hopeful. It wouldn't be wise to get too attached to our neighbors and rely on them. But while they offered to help Ella and me to get used to Fayette—and come to terms with the property that hosted a mystery—I'd take it.

Chapter Eight

Fortunately, the wind died down sometime this morning while we chatted in the kitchen. It wasn't warm by any means. The two-minute walk from Barbara and Ingrid's house was chilly, and I made a note to ask Barbara where she got her thick, puffy coat from.

I'd always let Ella make her own clothing choices, and a creature of comfort, she'd selected her coat for warmth rather than straight-up fashion. I'd wanted a puffier coat, but my mother-in-law gave me such a hard time about it, claiming it was too utilitarian, I'd returned it and got the same old thing—not warm enough but chic.

I am so *glad none of them will ever comment on what I wear. Ever again!* Reminding myself of that freedom, I couldn't help but grin as we walked over the driveways and winter-dead grass. We seemed to all have the same thought of *not* looking in the direction of the shed, and walking over here with blinders on seemed to bolster my confidence that Ella and I could make a home here.

"It kind of ruins your warm, peppy vibe," Ella commented of Barbara's coat I'd admired. While it looked warm, the dark-navy hue did not complement her attire. She held her head up regally as I unlocked the back door.

Once we stepped in, she opened her coat and flung it off, like a star entering a stage and losing her cloak of darkness. "But, now," she proclaimed mightily to the empty house, "I will reveal myself as the spot of sunshine I am!"

I gagged, pulling my collar from my neck at the nauseatingly intense heat.

"I thought the furnace was broken," Ella said, panting. She hurried to get her coat off, letting her gloves fall to the ground.

"Jeez."

Barbara whistled and she bunched up her coat and set it on a ledge in the mudroom. "And who told you it was broken?"

"That cop," I said, peering around the first room we'd entered, pleased at how spacious it seemed. Ella and I didn't need a lot of square footage. After leaving Blane's mansion, I was looking forward to not walking acres just to cross from the bedroom to the kitchen. Something small and cozy.

"Baby face?" Barbara said with a chuckle. "He only started on the force a few weeks ago. Fresh out of the academy."

"Yeah." I left my coat with Barbara's, stepping further into the house. "He said he tried to turn on the furnace. Fiddled with the thermostat."

"He didn't *fiddle* with it. He cranked it too high!" Ella whined, fanning herself.

"Oh, he means well," Barbara said. "I doubt he's owned a house to know much about them yet."

I led the way to the thermostat, which didn't make sense. Only set to sixty, it should have commanded the furnace to a low heat. Not a sauna. Our next step was to check the furnace, and it was there that we three gals decided it was malfunctioning beyond our limited scope of knowledge. We also concluded it was on the fritz to a level we were clueless, such that we didn't want to change anything and make it worse. Barbara shared numbers with me, and she immediately texted me the contact info for the HVAC company they swore by.

After that, we enjoyed ourselves checking out the house. Like the one next door, it was deceivingly roomier than the front suggested. Ella almost seemed giddy about having the room at the back, a balcony all to herself. I was content with the other bedroom, and as we walked through, I envisioned where my furniture could fit.

Before he'd passed, Fred truly had updated the house. The inside of it, at least, with the exception of the furnace. Newly refinished hardwood floors, replacement windows, fresh paint.

"I don't think he wanted to sell it," Barbara said, a helpful source of information about the house, having seen the workers come and go from next door. "But he'd felt it would be nice to leave something not so derelict? I don't know. But it sure looks move-in ready."

Once we'd adjusted the colors from white to a jade green in Ella's room, that was. Ever worried that she would be a materialistic brat, I was relieved when her only critique was that her bedroom walls made the room like clinical with all white. I could handle purchasing a gallon of paint, and I agreed. I was thinking maybe a nice naturally calming sandalwood hue for my room.

One day. I wasn't picky. Having a home without Blane in it was a utopia in its simplest form.

As we gathered our coats to leave, chancing the front door rather than the back since the tall maple tree wasn't dropping hazardous branches in the calm weather today, we lined up. We didn't zip our coats, but as we pushed our arms through the sleeves, we stepped out into the chillier air.

"Whew!" Barbara flapped her coat like fanning the cold air close. "That feels good."

"Hot flash?" Ella teased.

"Ella!" I scolded, embarrassed at her snark. She needed to learn to shut her little mouth!

Her cheeks turned even pinker, not from a flush of the too-hot house we'd left but likely embarrassment. Served her right. How dare she just mouth off like that? It wasn't funny at all.

"Sorry," she murmured.

Barbara only laughed. "Oh, honey. I've been there, done that. Menopause was a decade ago." She elbowed her. "But your mom's right. Had you said that to some other older woman, someone not as laidback and chill as me…" She slanted her brows in a stern frown of disapproval.

"Sorry…" Ella repeated, her cheeks even darker now.

"Oh, hey. No worries. Not for me. But I bet that attitude's a headache for her," Barbara said, tipping her chin at me as I locked the door. "So, Ingrid and I will help you curb it. Not lose it. But refine it."

"Please," I said honestly. "Her only other influence came from my in-laws. And that woman…"

Barbara giggled, patting my shoulder as I struggled to jimmy the key out of the lock. "I get the idea. But those in-laws are in the past now, right? Now it's time for Ingrid and me to pretend we're grandmas."

"You can be her fairy godmothers," I said dryly, narrowing my eyes at Ella as I finally got the key free. "Wave a wand and spare us all the misery that comes in the company of a moody teenager— Oh!" I started, turning around at a postwoman standing on the steps.

She smiled, but her face was so pinched while one cheek bulged that I wondered if she was sucking on a sour candy.

"Alexa," Barbara said, facing away from the house now. "Hello, honey."

"Yeah. Hi." Alexa shifted the messenger-style bag of mail from her right hip to the other. "Y'all the ones moving here?" she asked me. Then she swapped a wad of gum from her left cheek to the right, chomping loudly and straining her jaw on the size of the lump.

Boy, she was curt.

"Yes, I'm Naomi Front and this is my daughter, Ella." I thrust out my hand for an introductory shake, but she sniffed, ignoring my polite gesture and looking at Ella instead.

"You a junior? Or a senior?" she asked instead.

Ella didn't seem pleased about the mail lady's snub of my introduction. Or she wasn't impressed at the woman's almost snotty expression. She crossed her arms and gave the woman a slow once-over. "I don't give out personal information to strangers."

The lady raised her brows, perhaps not expecting what might have come across as sass. Unlike Ella's unwise "joke" about a hot flash to Barbara, I was proud of her answer. And prouder yet that she seemed able to read a person so well.

I wouldn't tell you anything either.

"This is Alexa Krogen," Barbara said. "She's been delivering the mail on this side of town for a few years now."

Even still, I didn't like her instantly snide attitude. Nor the way she checked out my daughter like she was a problem.

"If you're going to try for cheerleading, the captain spot's taken. Just so ya know," Alexa said haughtily, still seeming to size my daughter up. Almost like competition.

"We'll see about *that*, lady," Ella said. "Auditions aren't until the end of the month."

I turned, giving Alexa my back to stare at Ella and mouth, "What?!" She despised the idea of cheerleading, her opinion about sports and clubs—other than debate—awfully low.

Ella didn't have a chance to answer me, keeping her face in that stony stare teenagers perfected.

Alexa spoke up again. "Look here, *new girl*, my daughter's been the assistant captain of the team every year. Bree's gonna be captain. You hear?" She slapped mail into my hands, glaring a bit. "You gonna need to update your address at the office."

Then she turned, mumbling under her breath, to exit down the steps.

"I'm sorry about your loss," Barbara called out. She sounded sincere but it didn't carry the warmth she'd used when speaking with us or Ingrid. More like she felt she had to say it out of a societal obligation in passing.

Alexa froze mid-step, her shoulders stiffening before she turned back to glower at us. "Loss for what?" she scoffed.

"For your sister's death," Barbara replied.

Chapter Nine

Her sister? Yasmin was sisters with this rude, snotty mailwoman?

"My sister?" Alexa retorted. "She was no sister of mine." Leaning to her side, like seeking out the shed from this angle, she huffed. "My sister. That woman ceased being my *sister* eighteen years ago."

Barbara raised her hands, almost in surrender. "I understand."

"You understand?" Alexa stepped closer, something like rage making her face redder, her breaths quicker, and her nostrils flare.

Ella edged to the side, blocking Alexa from reaching Barbara.

"You *understand*?" Alexa sneered again, chomping harder and faster on her gum. "You don't know anything."

"I understand you and Yasmin had a disagreement all that time ago. But blood is blood."

Seeming to rein in her temper, Alexa cackled, her face still scrunched in anger despite the sound of what should have been amusement. "Yeah. Blood *is* blood." Then she stormed off.

Once she left, switching her bag back and forth between her sides, I exhaled a long, hard breath.

"That was tense," I quipped, for a lack of anything better to say.

"She was Yasmin's sister?" Ella asked.

"Uh-huh," Barbara said.

None of us made any move to leave, standing there and watching as Alexa stomped up to Mrs. West's house before roughly shoving a large handful of colorful junk mail into her mail slot. She scowled at us again from Mrs. West's porch, then carried on down the street.

Ella spoke first. "And what's up her—"

I rolled my eyes. "Her sister just died," I said. "It's not unbelievable that she'd be…out of sorts."

"And it's very believable she doesn't care that her sister is dead," Barbara said. She shook her head, like snapping out of a reverie, and headed toward her house.

"They didn't get along?" I asked.

"They fought from the moment they were born," Barbara said. "Worse when they were teens. Then after graduation, it was like Alexa disowned her. Never spoke of her again. Like she'd ceased to exist." Barbara shrugged.

"What did Yasmin do then?" I asked. "Did she act like that about Alexa too?"

Barbara nodded. "But then, she was too busy to spend time with her sister or reach out to her. Yasmin had a steady job, she soon married Jasper. Alexa seemed…stuck. She had Bree, went through one boyfriend after another, and no real jobs until a few years ago, when she applied for the postal position."

"And after all those years of, what, resenting each other, Alexa still won't acknowledge Yasmin after her murder?" I shivered, shocked at the cold treatment.

"I bet she'd care if Yasmin had any money," Ella piped up. "And she'd want to get her hands on it as her relative."

Barbara slung her arm around her shoulders. "See, if we look past the grumpiness, there's a smart lady in here." She mussed her hair, almost like a kid might rub knuckles on another smaller peer's head. Ella smiled, though, and I was thrilled that our neighbor could change the mood to a brighter note. "Because that was *exactly* what I was thinking. I wonder if Alexa is aware she'd likely get whatever Yasmin had."

"Hold on there." I held up my hand, not so quick to jump to the same assumption. Having pored over countless forms and making sense of so much paperwork about my belongings, Blane's belongings, retirement allotments, alimony, and other official documents about what we wished to do as we split our things, this topic was fresh on my mind.

"If they were such enemies, I doubt Yasmin would include her in her will."

Chapter Ten

When we returned to Barbara's house, Ingrid was gone, off to purchase sugar, for one thing, among other necessities for the pantry. I was touched when she asked Ella for her opinion about what we should have for dinner.

I struggled with the worry we were overstaying our welcome, making these two change their plans. But when Ingrid challenged Ella to help her prepare a lasagna from scratch, I noticed the excitement my daughter fought to hide.

Maybe they're getting as much from this as we are, I wondered.

"Back before we bought this house together, Ingrid had this spell of finding a rebound," Barbara said as she hung up our coat. "Her husband had passed away unexpectedly. Oh, gosh." She paused, frowning at the ceiling as she seemed to think hard as Ella and I removed our coats. "That was what? Twenty-five years ago? A long, *long* time ago."

Jeez. I was only thirty-five and I didn't feel that old. Twenty-five years wasn't *that* long ago.

"She first dated the coroner. Then the chief."

Ella laughed. "Your cousin? That chief?"

Barbara scoffed. "No. Not him!" Then she cackled. "Oh, Ingrid and Mike Mooney. That's a laugh. No, she dated the chief before him. Anyway, she still kept in touch with him. And Adam, the coroner, too. I'll just bet you she's already asked them what they know about Yasmin's murder. And if she hasn't, she will." She bustled into the kitchen, having promised us a "real" London Fog to chase away the chill from standing outside. It sounded like an excuse to make tea to me, but who was I to turn down her hospitality?

"Let's not waste time wondering about Yasmin's will when we'll know the full scoop sooner than later." She winked, getting down to business with the tea.

Chapter Eleven

Ingrid hadn't returned by the time Barbara made us our London Fogs. Ella was a bigger fan than I was. It was too…sweet? Something wasn't right about it, but I wasn't complaining. It did perk me up.

Someone else, however, had arrived after our unsettling run-in with Alexa on our porch. He hadn't shown up to offer a scoop of gossip. If anything, Chief Mooney showing up meant we'd need to curb our chitchat about Yasmin LeFleur.

"I hope they're not filling your head with nonsense," the chief told me after Barbara let him in. "I imagine Ingrid is already categorizing suspects and diving into motives, all from the drama and rumors in town."

Ella had gone upstairs to the guestroom for peace and quiet while she concentrated on her turn at chess in an online game she'd joined last week. She'd started playing chess when she was ten, and I had yet to beat her—or come close. I'd leave her to her "nemesis" in Japan, a college professor who was determined not to let Ella best her.

"It's not *nonsense*," Barbara chided him. "London Fog."

He made a face of disgust. "You know I only drink coffee."

"Have you made progress on the case?" I asked before the cousins could squabble.

"Yes and no." He brushed his hand over his hair, sighing. "I heard plenty of people have been peeking at your property. Curious and all."

I nodded. "That's expected, isn't it?"

"Yes."

"But Roxana Cardis shouldn't be helping herself to snooping near the shed early in the morning…" Barbara said with a sly *I know something you don't* smirk.

"She was *on* the property?" he asked.

"Uh-huh. Just when your cruiser out front seemed to be driving down the road."

"Must have been watching the cruiser to know when to snoop," I added, crossing my arms and leaning against the kitchen counter.

"Don't worry, Ms. Front. The excitement will fade. You won't have to worry about trespassers."

For once, Barbara agreed with him. "This is usually a very quiet, boring street."

"The gawkers will move on. And it's not your shed that's a big part of the case. We can confirm she was not stabbed there. No blood to indicate she had been."

"That's…good," I settled on for a reply. It wasn't a fortune, but I felt slightly easier hearing that fact. Yasmin had been deposited there. *Hidden?* Maybe so. The one door had been shut and the wind might have knocked the other open. And with Uncle Fred already gone for a few months, and the house uninhabited until Ella and I arrived, it likely did seem like a decent place to stash someone.

I was glad I didn't have to think a killer was choosing my home as a place to commit murder, but I wasn't crazy about accepting the fact someone had selected my shed as a dumpsite, either.

"Another reason I wanted to stop by and update you is that we had an incident with the shed. Georgie might have reversed into the shed door when he was transporting the body to the morgue. And well…he bumped it good." He finished with a sheepish wince.

I furrowed my brow and leaned over to glance out the window. It hadn't looked crooked when Barbara, Ella, and I walked over earlier, but then we'd been trying *not* to dwell and look that way. "It seems to be standing…"

"Sure, sure. It is. But, uh, honestly, I expect the whole thing's about to fall over."

Barbara sniffed, putzing around the kitchen. "Then you best be paying her some damages."

"It's about to fall over!" he protested.

I raised my hand, again to settle the peace between them. "That's not a priority. Besides, I'll probably have it demolished as soon as my budget allows."

"Now this business about Roxana," he said to Barbara. "Was she carrying anything? Looking for something?"

Barbara tilted her head. "What could she be looking for?"

He smiled all knowingly while he shook his head and wagged a finger at her. "Nah, nah, nah. That's not how this works. I'm not telling you that."

Barbara rolled her eyes and crossed her arms. "No. She wasn't carrying anything. But she did look like she wanted to go in the shed. Kept looking around in case anyone was watching her."

"Hmm." Chief Mooney rubbed his chin. "Pretty risky of her. Especially after she'd flat out asked me what would happen to Yasmin's personal effects and what she might have had in her pockets."

Something small enough to fit in a pocket, huh? Her wallet? Her phone? A receipt? A note? I was bitten by the snoopy bug of curiosity too.

"However, as Officer Rivera and Donn made clear to her when she stopped at the station last night, Yasmin's personal effects will not yet be disclosed as they are considered evidence to the case. And Yasmin's will is being reviewed as well, so don't bother hoping for details about that."

"It seems Roxana wanted to double back and make sure nothing was left behind," Barbara said.

"Is there any reason she could be a threat?" I asked him.

Barbara scoffed. "Well, she's one of *my* suspects in this case." She raised a brow at me. "We'll keep an eye on her if she thinks to trespass again."

Chief Mooney sighed. "A threat? No. But she has no right to trespass on your property. Should you see her lurking nearby again—or anyone setting foot on your property that you don't invite—you let us know."

"Oh, I'll handle it," Barbara said.

"You will not. If she becomes a suspect in the case, this is no laughing matter, Barbara."

"*Becomes?*" she snapped. "How could she not be on your list? Everyone knows how she fought with Yasmin about that failed pet photography thing."

"Because she has an alibi," he bit off. "And that's all I'll be sharing with you. Ms. Front, I just wanted to update you, and ask, again, if you see anything suspicious to please call us immediately. The patrols will stay nearby and check out the street's activities, but it wouldn't be a bad idea if you wanted to install surveillance cameras. At your earliest convenience, of course." He shrugged.

"I'll consider it." *Another expense to file in…* "But I can move in, right?"

"Sure, sure. The house itself is not part of the crime scene. And I apologize on behalf of Fayette if you're receiving more than usual attention for a while."

"If she busts down the shed, I bet that'll get rid a lot of the nosy ones stopping and gawking." Barbara gave me a thumbs-up with a hopeful smile.

We saw the chief out, and I turned to Barbara. "Is her TV *that* bright?"

She huffed. "Wait 'til you and Ella settle in. It'll be dang bright from your back windows. Even through curtains, unless you but some fancy black-out things with no seams."

"Fixing the furnace, trimming that tree, demolishing a shed, black-out curtains…" I shook my head, leaning my head against the back of the closed door. "And I haven't even had a chance to look for a job yet."

She blew a raspberry. "That's easy."

"Which part?"

"All of it." She returned to the kitchen, and I followed her, realizing this cozy tea-decorated room was a preferred spot to sit and chat. "Call Gin and I bet your furnace will be fixed by nightfall. That tree? File a request to the city council. That's on city space, so it's their responsibility. What else…demolishing the shed?" She shrugged. "Nothing a few sledgehammers and a dumpster can't solve on a warmer day. And if you duct tape around the cracks of normal windows, I'm sure the TV light won't be so bad in a pinch." She held her hands out, as though to say *see, nothing to fuss about.*

"And the job?"

She snapped her fingers. "Paul."

I raised my brows. "Who's Paul?"

"Assistant principal at the high school. He mentioned before school let out for winter break that the secretary at the front office was going on maternity leave, and the staff agency replacement quit. You can handle computers and a phone, right?"

"Who doesn't, to some degree?"

"Exactly. So there you go." She mimed dusting her hands off.

"There I go? That's just a possibility of a job vacancy. Not a guarantee."

"Oh, sure it is. I'll put a good word in. He's a sweetheart. Ingrid thinks the world of him too."

I sighed. "I suppose I could inquire about it. The first lead I've heard since we arrived."

Barbara plucked a grape from the fruit stand on the counter. "And what an arrival."

"But first, I need to move some things in. Ella and I can't take advantage and stay again."

"Oh, hush. She popped another grape into her mouth. "I thought you'd delegated me an honorary fairy godmother. I know we just met and all, honey, but…" She stood up, shrugging. "I'm excited. At first, Ingrid and I thought it'd be a young family moving in next door. Screaming toddlers and toys all over the yard. But Ella's…"

I leaned my forearms on the counter to peer at her. "Yes, tell me your opinion of the sassy teenager who thought to tease you about having a hot flash."

She chuckled. "Well, she's sweet. How she stood up to Alexa, defensive of you. Doesn't take trouble but delivers her own. She's got grit. And heart. If I had to be poetic about it, she's kind of like the granddaughter I never had."

I sighed, smiling at her. "And I *know* she's never had a grandmotherly figure to look up to. My mother passed away when I was her age. And Blane's mother…"

Barbara giggled, holding up a hand to stop me. "I get the picture. What I'm trying to say is I enjoy your company, hers too. Don't feel like you need to rush out of here just when we're getting used to you two."

"Thank you, Barbara. But we really do need to hurry and get some stuff in the house. Hot-and-cold furnace or not, I need to return that rental truck before the bill is sky-high."

"How about this, then? My yoga class was canceled, and I'm caught up on the series I was binge-reading. I can call Gin about the heater and then text Paul about that position. Then I'll come and help you two bring things in." She raised her arm, flexing her muscles. "I may be old, but I got some life in these guns." Patting her bicep, she grunted, like a tough hulk. "I stay in shape, you know. Cuz if you don't use it, you'll lose it."

I giggled before I rounded the counter to hug her. "Thanks, again, Barbara."

"That's what friends are for—even newfound ones." She saluted me before snatching her phone from the counter and walking away. "I'll report to duty in about an hour, okay?"

AUBREY ELLE

A SPOT OF EARL SLAY

Chapter Twelve

"Does Dad know about Yasmin's body being dumped here?"

That was Ella's first question as we began to carry her things into the house. *Her* things, because she'd wanted to keep her bedroom furniture set. I saw nothing wrong with that. It was a big adjustment to relocate from the home she'd grown up in, and if I had the power to see to it, I'd keep things as consistent as possible. Which meant bringing her bed, chair, desk, and dressers with us.

My things would arrive soon. I'd used some of the alimony to purchase a new bedroom set since I refused to take anything in Blane's house. For now, Ella and I could share a room.

101

"I imagine he does, since Chief Mooney confirmed our alibis with the hotel staff." I'd been staying there with Ella while Blane and I separated for the month before the divorce was finalized.

"And Dad knows the manager, who probably blabbed to him," she said, hefting the other end of her chair as she walked up the steps.

"Uh-huh." Since Barbara hung up on him this morning, he'd called countless times. I'd set the phone to silent, but I wouldn't block his calls. If I did that, he'd likely use it against me for his useless, halfhearted case of getting custody of Ella. He only wanted it to bother me, not that he wanted to suddenly act like her father.

"I'll have to fill him in on the details sooner or later." *But not today. Too many things to do today.*

She rolled her eyes. "I bet Grandmother is having a fit."

"When isn't she, though?"

Ella smiled, shaking her head. "Again, Mom. I don't know how you put up with them for so long and stayed sane."

Because he wasn't outright abusive to me. Because I wanted to provide the best I could for you. Which ended up being far from what I had done, subjecting her to a loveless home.

"What was with that cheerleading stuff earlier?" I asked her once we'd climbed the steps to the porch. "With Alexa," I clarified.

She scoffed. "What about it?"

"You don't want to be a cheerleader."

"Ugh." She grimaced. "Please, no."

"Then why'd you say that you knew when auditions were?"

"I wanted to mess with her. She came on so strong, acting all mighty, like Bree will get that captain whatever title handed to her just because she says so." She laughed. "I wanted to knock her off her pedestal."

As I'd suspected she had. "Were you making it up about the auditions?"

"No." She squealed when she almost lost her hold on the chair as we turned for the stairs to the second floor. "I saw it on the school page. They are hosting auditions soon." She rolled her eyes as we brought the chair up the stairs.

"Careful. Don't knock it into the wall," I cautioned.

"It was kind of weird, too."

"What was?"

"For starters, how *big* of a deal cheerleaders are. I looked up the basketball and football team stats, to see if they were good, and if they'd want their cheer team to match that skill level. Um, not. The football team hasn't even gone past city championships. Last year, the basketball team almost reached regionals, but the half-back got busted with a DUI."

I frowned. I was a cross-country runner way back when, but I remembered going to some games. "Half-back? I think that's soccer."

"Whatever. Some so-called star got busted and they didn't advance after all because he couldn't play."

Yet more points against her new school. Oh, joy.

"But they treat the cheerleaders like they're celebrities. In fact, that Bree girl? She made some huge comment about auditions, basically saying she wishes everyone luck but so sorry they lost. Like, really. And her boyfriend or whoever he is, he jumps on, praising her for her so-called selfless consideration and good sportsmanship to extend good wishes to others who wanted to make the cheer squad—even though no auditions have been held!"

I sighed, struggling for something to say. She was above that kind of petty drama, but I wasn't sure how to talk her down from coming across as inferior and judgmental.

"*And,*" she added dramatically, not done with her rant yet as we reached the landing at the top of the stairs. "He's like super creepy and old, trying too hard to look like a bad-boy rebel."

"This boyfriend?"

"I think. I saw them in tons of pictures together."

"Just how old are you talking?" I asked, worried about a predator or some wacko grooming teenagers.

"Not *that* old. But older than a teenager. Like twenty? He just looked so much older than her, especially in that cheerleading costume. She was even wearing it in one picture, where he'd posted he lost his job, his boss, some Jameson guy, was a class-a jerk to him... Some pity story."

I jerked up. "You mean that guy who wants people to 'donate' to him because he *quit* his job and doesn't want to get another one? The PleaseFundMe posts?"

"Yeah! That's the same guy talking up Bree. Mark something," she said. "Look, Mom. I'm really going to try. I want to be openminded and accept this place as my new home."

"For now, at least," I added. I didn't want to hold her back. If she wanted to go somewhere specific for college—an as-of-yet undetermined choice—I'd support that and follow her there. To someone looking in, they'd probably think I'd lived the last eighteen years conforming to Blane's wishes, and now I'd be switching to be a slave to what Ella wanted. But that wasn't true. It didn't take me much to be happy. I spent the last seventeen years doing what I felt best for her, and isolated in that toxic family, it'd more or less become Ella and me against the world. Partners.

"Really? You wouldn't want to stick around?"

I had to laugh as we set the chair down in her room. "We have had an unconventional time since we got here." *How was that only yesterday?* It felt like so much longer.

"Barbara and Ingrid are cool, though," she said as she left the room to get the next item from the moving van.

I smiled, trailing after her. *You're not wrong about that, girlie.*

"I'll try, Mom. I'll really give this place a chance, but if that Mark guy and Bree are representatives of the peers of this area..." She sighed, shaking her head.

"Don't tell me you're too good to suffer fools," I teased.

She rolled her eyes.

For the next hour or so, we carried in the majority of her furniture—fortunately, her dressers and bed were unassembled. And as particular as Ella was about things, she insisted she'd be in charge of re-assembling. Because she was practically an independent woman now, not a child.

We also carried in a few furniture pieces and appliances I had ordered before leaving Swenton, storing them at the hotel's basement space. Chairs, a side table, and a floor lamp to go into the living room. Then a microwave, coffeemaker, and toaster for the kitchen.

As we worked as a team, flipping between the wintery chill outside and the too-hot house, I told her I might have a job at the high school. I'd anticipated her to roll her eyes or show some other form of annoyance at me being there, but she didn't seem to care. Her priority was making sure we were finished with the moving van before Ingrid could show her how to make that lasagna.

"What about a car?" Ella asked as we headed outside for more boxes.

"What about a car?" Barbara parroted. She walked toward us, the sunshine-yellow getup replaced with casual jeans and a sweatshirt. In clothes I bet she wouldn't mind getting dirty or sweaty as she helped us empty the van.

"I'll need one. As soon as I return the van, I'll hunt for something." I smiled at her, catching my breath from carrying in those boxes of books. "I didn't want the headache of dealing with Blane and that darn BMW. I planned on getting something used around here."

"Well, you can borrow mine for now. Paul says the schools are closed."

Ella scoffed. "Yeah, it's winter break."

"No, the admin offices too. Some updating they're doing to the computers or running more wires for routers. Something." She shrugged one shoulder. "But he said he'll be at the café on Main Street in about fifteen minutes. He said he could print off the forms and chat with you there."

I raised my brows. "You mean interview me?"

Barbara smirked. "Oh, don't worry. I put in a good word for you."

"You hardly know me!"

"But I will." She walked up the van's ramp. "And I know you've got to be a saint and smart woman to have raised this fine young lady," she gushed, hugging Ella to her side. My daughter might have wanted to stay cool, but I saw how happy she was at the affection, smiling at the side hug.

"My keys are hanging on the last hook on the rack above the mail slot flap. Go on, go on."

I peered at her driveway, further back. A black sedan waited. "You sure?"

"She said to go on, Mom." Ella paused to instruct Barbara which boxes should be moved next. "Hurry. So we can get onto the lasagna tonight."

I backpedaled, raising my hands. "Hey. That's on *you*. I thought you were making it for us."

"Go, Mom, go." She smiled as she practically shooed me away. Almost like she was eager to spend time with Barbara instead of me.

Like...getting used to the idea of what having a grandma would be like. I grinned, confident she would be fine with Barbara.

Yet as I crossed the driveways to retrieve Barbara's keys, I couldn't help but glance at the shed where someone had thought to dump Yasmin's body.

Just like that, my mood soured again.

They just had to pick that *shed to hide her in? Of all the houses and yards and garages and sheds on the street, why that one? Why me?* Hadn't I faced enough trouble lately?

As soon as I thought it, I stopped, frowning as I took in the backyard area.

It wasn't like me to fret and feel down for the sake of some superstitious silliness, like fate was making my life hard for the heck of it.

Why did *they choose that shed?*

Knowing I had fifteen minutes to while away, I walked around Barbara's house to peer into the backyard and scope it out.

For that matter, how did they get the body in the shed?

I glanced back at the pavement. *Back up down the driveway?* Squinting, I looked further back, across the street. Even from here, I saw the telltale box on their doorway. A security camera. Chief Mooney had to have checked that feed for something as simple as that. If someone had backed down Uncle Fred's driveway and left Yasmin, the footage would show the car.

No. That'd be too obvious, wouldn't it? I resumed exploring the backyard. Ella and I had an old privacy fence facing the back end. To the right, a row of bushes blocked us from Mrs. West's yard, which also had a rear privacy fence.

In Ingrid and Barbara's yard, though, I saw past their gardens, spotting a shorter, split-rail type fence running along the back. I walked closer, careful not to step in a flower bed or some sort of ceramic statue of art. Almost past what looked like an intensive vegetable garden, wired cones for trailing plants and weathered, faded images of cucumbers and carrots still attached to markers in the hard dirt, I saw the path.

A slim alley ran along the back, and after noticing garbage cans with the Fayette logo screen-printed on them, I figured it must be a garbage route for the houses backed up to each other.

"Hmm…" Still careful of where I stepped, lest I crunch a plant, I poked through the shrubs and reached where Barbara and Ingrid kept their trash cans.

Looking one way, then the other, I saw nothing but residences. Nothing out of the ordinary.

But it sure looks like anyone could drive up this alley.

And perhaps this route was how someone had delivered Yasmin to the most worn-down and rickety shed at what appeared to be an abandoned house.

Chapter Thirteen

Barbara's car was comfortable but I questioned her choice of an air freshener. I got the point. Those ladies loved their tea, something I wanted to ask about. How'd they get so many teacups and teapots? What started it? Why tea instead of coffee? There were *no* coffee beans in that house. I assumed people began collecting certain items for a reason. Or maybe it was all just a whim.

The air freshener reminded me too much of a citrus sort of drink rather than an air purifier.

"Not that it's any of my business," I whispered to myself as I backed up.

As I reversed, I spotted Ella and Barbara carrying boxes. My daughter spoke animatedly and our neighbor seemed to struggle with her balance between cracking up and maintaining a hold on her box.

Smiling once more, I was determined to make today a better one than yesterday.

Grateful that Fayette was a small town, I easily found my way toward Main. Parking wasn't terrible, and after a short walk down the sidewalks, I faced the entrance to the one and only café in town.

Only a few customers sat at tables, but the lack of a crowd didn't help. I hadn't thought to ask Barbara what this Paul man would look like, and I was so busy moving things into the house that I hadn't taken a chance to check him out online.

"Naomi?" A chair scooted back to my right, the legs scraping loudly on the tile floor. "Ms. Front?" he called out the second time.

I turned, smiling at the tall stranger. *No, I've seen him before. He's the runner the paper wrote about, some challenge to do all of the state's charity 5K runs this year—not a teacher, but the assistant principal, it seems.*

As soon as we made eye contact, he grinned and lifted his hand in a wave. The gesture almost seemed cheesy, shy even, and it made me wonder if that was what offering my hand for a shake was like for me. A nervous tic of knowing I should do something to streamline a hello or introduction, so why not thrust my hand out as quickly as possible for a shake?

With that odd thought on my mind, I fought the urge to accost him for an immediate handshake after I approached. Instead, I mirrored him and gave a little wave.

No. That wasn't right either. I felt like a teenager. *My gosh, did living with Blane make me a social ditz.*

"Hi. I'm Paul."

Barbara must have told him what I looked like for him to spot me so quickly, and I couldn't help but wonder how she'd described me. Jeans, a long-sleeve shirt, my hair…maybe in a bun still. I hadn't even thought to shower beforehand, that was how rusty I was with the idea of interviewing for a job. Then again, I hadn't been allowed the time to freshen up.

"Nice to meet you." And there went my hand. Only I overestimated how far I was and smacked his coffee over. "Oh!" I cringed, darting closer to mop up the spill with the napkins from the dispenser.

His chuckle was kind. He wasn't laughing at me as he tried to help me wipe it and set the cup upright again. Finished, the table not shiny with liquid but probably still sticky, I sighed and faced him again.

"Well, that was a stellar first impression."

He simply smiled again. What a smile it was. Gentle and warm, like his face was used to laughing and enjoying life. Carefree and open. I had the immediate guess Paul would be a laidback and easy-to-please man. "Don't worry about it." He gestured for me to sit, and I schooled myself from keeping my motions smooth and graceful as I did. "After what you've probably experienced in the last day or two, I'd be skittish too."

The last day or two? I wanted to laugh. I'd been stressed longer than that.

"So, Barbara insists you're the only woman for this job," he said as a waitress brought over a new cup of coffee for him. I declined, feeling that it would be a betrayal to my tea-obsessed neighbors somehow.

"And she's only known me for less than forty-eight hours!" I said.

"She's just one of those rare gems. A good friend and an even better judge of character." Paul relaxed in his chair, leaning back and crossing his leg to rest his ankle on the other knee. "I'll take her word for it. If she likes you, I'll li—" He smiled, pausing abruptly. After a deep breath, perhaps to stop while he was ahead, he said, "If she trusts you, I'll trust you."

Huh. That was nice. Taking someone's word of mouth and opinion as the basis of a judgment. Not what they drove, where they vacationed, and how much they donated to charities to balance their owed taxes.

He got right to business, explaining the expectations of the secretary position. I was honest, admitting what computer programs I did and did not have experience with.

"Are you familiar with a fax machine?" he asked. He'd grabbed a slim notebook from a laptop bag resting by his feet. Pausing in jotting notes about my replies, he looked up at me, brows raised.

A what now? I licked my lips. "Uh… People still use those?"

He laughed, a rich, hearty sound that had me smiling in an instant. Still, I didn't get the idea that he was making fun *of* me, just finding little things to *have* fun. "I'm messing with you. No, we don't use them."

"Whew."

"I wanted to see if you'd lie to impress me."

I shrugged. "What good would telling you do me when proving my inexperience would show it?"

He nodded, seeming pleased with my answer. "Actions do speak louder than words."

Another nugget of lofty wisdom that couple's counselor had espoused to Blane and me. He'd let it in one ear and out the other.

"I'm confident I can impress you in other ways."

I froze as soon as I said it. *Is that— Was that—* I swallowed hard. *Was that flirting?*

He smiled, raising his brows. "Oh, yeah?"

I couldn't tell how he'd taken that statement. Flirting? Jeez. I couldn't think back to the last time I had. Or if I ever tried to. Blane was my first, and I hadn't been outgoing enough to date before him. *Oh, no…* I hadn't intended to hit on him!

"Tell me then. Why should I give you this job?"

I licked my lips. That sounded professional, not pervy. Or like flirting. *Does flirting have specific criteria? No. It can't. That's why men and women miscommunicate so often.*

He peered at me, waiting patiently.

"One, because I'm a single mom of a teenager," I lifted one finger to count it off. "Which means I'm familiar with teenage behavior."

"Ella, right?"

I nodded. "Two, because I'm brave."

He lifted one corner of his mouth in consideration, sitting back again. "That's a bold claim."

"Yep. I'm brave because I had the guts to divorce my ex."

His frown came so fast I looked over my shoulder, wondering if someone he disliked had entered the café. "Was he abusive?"

"No, no, no. Nothing like that. His family was toxic, but I could handle him." I rolled my eyes. "Until I didn't want to put up with any of them. So, that took guts. And I was brave to leave."

"True. That is a brave thing to do."

"You're divorced?" Again, as soon as I said it, I closed my eyes and wondered if I wasn't too old to blush. He'd said it so surely, like he'd experienced it himself. "Sorry. That's none of my business."

"Never married. I moved here for the assistant principal position straight out of college—which I was late to graduate from because I was in the Navy. Go on. How else can you impress me?"

"Two. No, I'm on three. Okay. Three, I have experience keeping track of documents, making calls, and arranging schedules." I shrugged. "For a household, but it's the same thing."

"Good. Good."

I raised a fourth finger. "And I'm determined to make this work." I was reaching here, but I wasn't lying. Paul didn't seem like someone I'd want to lie to. He had that open kind of personality, like it'd be a crime to ruin his easy trust.

"I moved here so Ella and I could have a fresh start. But since we showed up, it's been…well, rocky. But I haven't truly given a thought to leaving and escaping the hard times." I nodded, hoping that sounded positive rather than pathetic. "As in, I'm not a quitter when times get tough," I added for clarification.

"I can only imagine." He closed his notebook, leaning in like he wanted to whisper instead. "I thought the newspaper deliverer was lying, spreading a rumor—"

"A *paper* newspaper?" I crinkled my nose, amused. "People still read those?"

"*I* do." He chuckled. "Doubles for puppy potty training liners, too. At least I can't admit to having a fax machine."

I giggled, thinking this was too much fun to be a real interview. Teasing, joking, and laughing with a man…

Wait. This is *an interview.* No matter how charming he was, I had to keep my head on straight here. It was light years too soon to consider something with a man. The ink on my divorce papers was still drying!

"I thought the newspaper deliverer was spreading a rumor about a dead body found at old Fred's house. But when I passed by on my run this morning, I figured the crowd of people clearly staring at your house meant something really had happened."

"Chief Mooney assured me she wasn't killed there," I was quick to add, like I didn't want my new home to suffer from the connotation of being a killer hotspot. "Just…left there."

"So Barbara said, too, when she called earlier."

A worry flitted through my mind. "Wait a second. You're not giving me this job out of pity, are you?" I narrowed my eyes and tapped my finger on the table. "Because I might be struggling a little at the moment, I'm not too proud to deny that. But I don't want a handout. I don't want charity."

"Who says I am giving you the job?" he asked, his tone teasing.

I clamped my lips shut and bit on them. *Foot, meet mouth.*

"Relax, relax." He leaned over to shove his notebook into his laptop bag. "Of course, you have the job." He proved it too, by sliding a bunch of forms to fill out for insurance and whatnot. I set them in my purse, glad for the bulk of paperwork. It was tangible proof I'd start a job soon!

"Not out of pity, though, right?" Even if I refused to consider the idea of flirting, dating, or seeking out a man for anything, I cared what he thought of me at this first impression.

"No. Because you're the only applicant and we need someone—anyone to start once break is over."

I furrowed my brow, not sure if that was better or worse than getting a job out of pity.

Again, he laughed. "I'm teasing, again."

I exhaled in relief. "Sorry. I'm usually not this slow to detect sarcasm."

He stood, so I did as well. "I'm offering you the job because I like to think I'm also a good judge of character. And so far, you *have* impressed me, Ms. Front."

Hearing a gentleman like him say my married name had me wincing. "Just Naomi is fine," I said. "Unless that's unprofessional."

He offered his hand for a shake now. "I look forward to working with you, Naomi."

I shook his hand. *More like working* for *you, boss.* "Thanks, Mr. Quinn."

"Just Paul," he corrected. He released my hand but grabbed it again when a loud bang sounded behind me. Pulling me to the side, as though to shield me from the sudden crash, he stared ahead.

Gasping, I turned just in time to witness a woman from across the café. Scowling, she shoved a man in his chest. He stumbled back, perhaps not for the first time. Behind him was an upturned table he must have bumped into when she'd pushed him to create that loud noise.

"No, Jasper," she shouted.

"But, Melissa," Jasper pled, reaching for her hand.

She growled, raising on her tiptoes and getting in his face. "I said no. I won't move in with you. I don't care if you got rid of her, I'm not moving in with you!"

Chapter Fourteen

Jasper stared, slack-jawed and paralyzed as Melissa flounced away, impatiently pushing the café's door open and nearly plowing over Chief Mooney and Officer Donn as they entered. Brows raised and eyes wide in surprise, Fayette's cops did a double-take as Melissa strode away from the café.

Officer Donn volleyed his gaze from Melissa hurrying down the sidewalk and stunned Jasper gaping after the woman. "What'd we miss?"

Chief Mooney stepped back out through the doorway, one foot in the café, and the other on the welcome mat outside. "Miss Varga?" he called after her.

As they stared after the woman who'd stormed off in a snit, they'd turned their backs to the occupants of the café. I couldn't see Melissa anymore, the wide wall of windows not showing that far down Main's sidewalk. Instead, I tried to slot her name into my mind, wondering why it sounded familiar despite never meeting her. It was hard, trying to fit in all the new names and details as I got used to Fayette. But I didn't have time to wonder about who she might be.

Jasper finally snapped out of his shell-shocked state of paralysis, slanting to the side. No, not a slant. He tilted further—falling.

"Watch his head!" I rushed ahead, realizing he was fainting. Paul darted forward with me, faster on his feet because he reached the stunned man first. He caught his back, falling to his knees and sliding over so Jasper didn't smack his head on the corner of the closest bistro table. I bumped my hip into a chair in the way, catching Jasper's shoulder to help steer him from the table as well.

"What in the…" Chief Mooney faced us now, forgetting about calling after that woman. "He fainted?"

I nodded, stepping back and letting Paul lower him the rest of the way to the black and white checkered floor.

"Looks like it," Paul said, moving aside as Chief Mooney and Officer Donn crowded closer, taking charge.

I scooted chairs back so the men could have room to assess Jasper. The server who'd filled Paul's coffee approached, helping me to nudge the bistro table back. "Do you need anything, Officers?" she asked, alarm and worry clear on her face. "Should we clear room for an ambulance to pull up at the front?"

As she spoke, though, Jasper stirred. He tried to sit up, moaning a little. "Oh…" He raised his hand—the movement smooth and direct for someone who'd passed out—and patted the back of his head. "Oh… that hurt."

I narrowed my eyes at him. Paul frowned too, catching my gaze. "What hurt?" he asked.

"Didn't you see? I bumped my head." Jasper shook it now, like trying to clear the fog, but his eyes seemed awfully clear and focused for someone who'd just fainted and miraculously recovered.

"No, you didn't," I argued and pointed at Paul and myself. "We caught you so you *wouldn't* knock your head."

"No. I'm sure I knocked my head…"

I opened my mouth to protest. He was lying!

"Save the theatrics for another time, LeFleur," Chief Mooney said tiredly. "You got a whole room of witnesses who can say otherwise."

LeFleur! This was Yasmin's ex? What I remembered the most from what Barbara and Ingrid said of him, he was a dog-loving, anti-cat man who argued with his ex-wife. The attractive, fit guy struggling to sit up surprised me. He was more good-looking than I'd thought he might be, and as he sheepishly smiled at Chief Mooney, I noticed his charisma.

Too much charisma. Like a conman. Overly sly and persuasive and getting others to agree with him by the force and wattage of his smile.

And a liar. A woman tasked with raising a headstrong teenager would not go far in life without building a trust BS detector. He hadn't fainted, not if he was as sharp and in charge of his faculties just like that!

"After that nonsense Melissa shouted at me…" Jasper shook his head again, gripping the seat of a chair to hoist himself up like he was a wounded, frail victim. "I can't tell what's what. I sure *feel* like I hit my head." Standing, he faced the waitress and held up his hand. "No need for an ambulance, sweetheart. I'm fine. Shaken." He patted the back of his head. "I'm shaken, but I'm fine. No need for an ambulance and their outrageous out-of-pocket fees."

Hmm. *Worried about money but not ready to admit he'd faked that faint and fall…* That faint was what, then? A ploy? A grab for attention or pity after Melissa shouting at him?

"What was Melissa going on about?" Chief Mooney asked him, glancing at me and Paul.

"She said"—I raised my fingers to air quote—"she won't move in with him. She doesn't care if he got rid of 'her', she still won't move in with him."

Jasper lost his charming suave smile to snarl at me. "And who are you? Poking your nose into my business."

Paul cleared his throat. "I heard the same." He gestured at the café. "Everyone did."

Jasper straightened his cuffs, chuckling weakly. "Well, you know what they say. The passionate women are always the loud ones."

I rolled my eyes.

"What was she talking about?" the chief asked, hands on his hips.

Crossing my arms, I settled in to eavesdrop on this answer. "As new as I am to all this drama, it sounded to me she was referring to Yasmin."

"What's it to you?" Jasper sneered.

I opened my mouth to reply, but Chief Mooney must have noticed the anger on my face. "All right. That's enough. Jasper? What was she going on about then?"

Jasper's scowl lost some of its intensity as he turned from me to face the cops. "She *was* talking about Yasmin. And I *did* get rid of her—by leaving her. Remember? I divorced her months ago. I left her to be with Melissa instead."

"If it was months ago, why is she shouting at you about it now?" I asked.

Chief Mooney shot me a look to shut up.

"Because Melissa doesn't let go of grudges that easily. Like I said, she's a passionate woman. She harbors passionate feelings. She feels *deep*." Jasper lightly tapped his fist at his chest, as if emphasizing his belief Melissa clung to heartfelt, strong emotions.

"And she deeply feels that she'll never move in with you?" I asked.

Again, he glowered at me. "Who the heck *are* you?"

"Okay, okay. Let's move this along." That's enough, Ms. Front." Chief Mooney raised his voice to address the still-quiet crowd who hung on Jasper's every word. "Drama's over. Lovers' spat. Nothing to see here." Then he faced him. "Nothing to see here, right, Mr. LeFleur?"

Jasper huffed. "No. Nothing at all. We were just…arguing." He walked off but then doubled back. "Like I said yesterday, I did *not* kill Yasmin. I never wanted to stay married to her, but I didn't loathe her so much I'd end her life."

Standing straighter and puffing out his chest, he held his head high and exited the café.

After he left, I huffed a laugh. "You're not just going to take his word for that, are you?"

Chief Mooney got into line, rolling his eyes. "No, I am not."

"I'll catch up with you later, Naomi," Paul said, lifting his hand to show me his ringing cell. "I've got to go and take this call, but I'll email you details about the position in a day or two."

"Thank you, Paul," I said as he took off hastily.

Officer Donn stepped into line after his boss, leaning around him to peer at the menu. "Jasper didn't do it, Ms. Front. I bet you want closure to the case that involves your property, but he ain't the one."

"Just because he says so? He seems like a classic liar."

A woman piped up behind the officers in line. "Jasper *is* a liar. He sure scammed me on that promise for a low-interest rate from the so-called insurance company he works for."

"Jasper LeFleur didn't kill Yasmin because he's too dainty to get his hands dirty stabbing her," another customer drawled, teasing from further up in line. He chuckled, shaking his head.

"That's enough," Chief Mooney said loudly, his baritone still just as tired. "This is an open investigation, and we are working on it."

"Convince me that I shouldn't worry about Jasper dumping another dead body at my home," I said. "He's got a motive. He could have a means—"

Officer Donn smiled, laughing at Chief Mooney's groan. "Barbara's been filling you with all kinds of chitchat about this, huh?" He frowned at me.

"Tell me he doesn't have the motive to kill her," I said. He clearly had no issue announcing how much he disliked his ex.

"I imagine he might have," Officer Donn said. "It sounds like Yasmin fought the divorce where he clearly wanted it. But in the end, they *did* finalize the separation for good."

"And he could have had the means," I said. Finding a knife wasn't hard. Every kitchen had at least one.

"If he was left-handed and had stolen a knife from the commercial bakery's storeroom," Chief Mooney argued. "Which he is not and did not."

My shoulders slumped, my argument fading. "Oh." *The commercial bakery? That's where he determined the weapon came from? Wilson Bakery?*

"Besides, he's got an alibi too," Officer Donn said, shrugging at me. "No opportunity for killing her."

"I'm not sure that alibi is credible, though," Chief Mooney countered, shooting his officer a side-eye before facing me again. "But no, Ms. Front. In my professional capacity, I don't think you have any reason to worry about Jasper LeFleur dumping a body on your property."

But someone else did. If not Jasper, then who?

AUBREY ELLE

Chapter Fifteen

As I drove home from the café, realizing I wasn't going to get anything else from Chief Mooney and Officer Donn as they ordered afternoon pick-me-ups of sugary coffees, I wondered out loud.

"Motive, means, and opportunity…"

I'd surprised myself, talking in proper mystery terms with Mooney and Donn. Ella and I had gone through a spell of binge-watching a spoof of a British murder mystery series. Great for slapstick humor and easy on the stressed mind. Of course, we'd only been able to sneak our viewing in when Blane wasn't home. Because he'd claimed it was "unpatriotic" to watch entertainment not based in the U.S.

I scoffed to myself, regret bubbling up once again. "How the heck did I stay with him for so long?"

As if on cue, my phone buzzed from the cupholder. Ella's name flashed in the ID, with a text that read, *Done with the moving van. Ingrid helped to empty it too. It appears I've adopted very strong grandmas.* She'd stuck a strong arm emoji at the end of it.

I smiled.

Ella. She was the reason I'd stayed in that loveless marriage. It was too bad that hadn't been the wisest option in the big picture of life, but we were here and resolutely moving on.

I shook my head, chasing away the blues that surfaced whenever I meandered down the line of regret-fueled thoughts.

"Okay. Motive, means, and opportunity," I repeated to myself.

Jasper LeFleur had a motive: loathing his ex. And the same general dislike applied to the two other people I'd heard about or met. It was no mystery Yasmin had plenty of enemies, and she seemed to welcome antagonism naturally.

Jasper likely loathed her from the conflict of a bad marriage. Understandable. My opinion of Blane was too high. Being married to a poor fit of a spouse was bound to simmer *a lot* of dislike and loathing.

Alexa Krogen fell into the category of disliking Yasmin. Her hatred seemed to run deeper, maybe a bad case of sibling rivalry? Something that seemed consistent throughout life, as according to Barbara, the mailwoman cut Yasmin out of her life long ago and still to this day didn't seem torn by her sister's death.

And the business partner. Roxana Cardis. She also fit in with the anti-Yasmin club. Her sentiments of dislike seemed rooted in another lack of compatibility. From what I could gather, Yasmin and Roxana were two acquaintances within Fayette who'd tried and failed to create a pet photography business. With what Ingrid shared about Roxana's rant at the post office, it seemed to me that perhaps Roxana's feelings about Yasmin were borne of a dispute about money. If Roxana ponied up and invested in the business plan that failed to come through, it made perfect sense she'd be impacted to the point her wallet suffered.

The means, though, I couldn't wrap my head around that.

Chief Mooney might not have intended to let me know about the knife coming from the commercial bakery, but that sure complicated my train of thought. That limited access to the particular knife used to stab Yasmin. Then again, maybe that wasn't true either.

While I had yet to stop at the commercial bakery, I did notice on the drive into town that a sign announced the hours of operation for a small shop attached to the bakery warehouse.

It wasn't too far of a reach to assume a customer could slip in and grab a knife. Heck, maybe it was a specific sort of knife the bakery sold as a novelty, with their logo imprinted on it. Because how else could Chief Mooney be so sure the knife came from the bakery?

Fingerprints?

I shrugged to myself.

As far as opportunity went, I wasn't sure how to compare the three I had at the forefront of my mind. The chief seemed to have accepted Roxana's alibi, whatever it was, but he'd been skeptical about Jasper's. I had no idea if Alexa had an alibi, either.

Too soon, I pulled into Barbara and Ingrid's driveway. A dark-gray SUV was parked in front of their garage, indicating Ingrid was indeed home. I glanced to the right, checking that Ella or the gals had closed the sliding door to the van. They'd resecured the padlock, too, saving me the time of having to do that. Even though our belongings were out, I didn't want to risk someone snooping and vandalizing the rental vehicle.

Or think it is a good spot to leave another dead body.

I stepped out of Barbara's sedan, eager to get inside and discuss my thoughts with Barbara and Ingrid.

Before I could, though, I narrowed my eyes at someone creeping from an opening in Barbara and

Ingrid's garden. Someone sneaking closer, headed for my shed.

I turned on the flashlight on my phone. It wasn't completely dark yet as dusk still approached, but shining the light worked just as I intended. The flash of brightness could have very well been a spotlight, catching the trespasser like a deer in headlights.

"And just what do you think you're doing?" I asked, hand on hip.

Roxana Cardis sighed, lowering her shoulders and muttering a curse.

AUBREY ELLE

Chapter Sixteen

"It's not what it looks like," the brunette said, raising her hands in surrender.

I shut off my phone's flashlight and intercepted her near the shed. She clearly wasn't holding a weapon, but I pressed the camera icon on my phone long enough to activate the video mode, just to capture whatever she'd offer me as an explanation.

"It looks like you're trespassing on my property when you shouldn't be."

She scoffed, pointing toward the grass. "I'm *not* on your property, actually, you big-city snob."

"Wanna bet Barbara and Ingrid won't be thrilled you're snooping back here?" I challenged, full of faith that even though our friendship and neighborly status were new, they'd side with me over this woman.

"Shh." Roxana shoved her hands in her pockets, frowning at me. "No one needs to know. Least of all blabbermouth Barbara. She'd be sure to tell Chief Mooney I'm here again, and I don't care for him breathing down my neck and trying to intimidate me anymore."

"Intimidate you?" I laughed once. "I think it's called 'investigating the murder of your former business partner.'"

"Partner?" she spat. "Yasmin was never my partner."

"Not what I heard."

Roxana rolled her eyes. "And what would you have heard, anyway? You just moved here!"

"I saw you and Yasmin on a business page. One you removed her from, too."

"Yeah, and I had every right to!" Roxana kicked the grass, shaking her head. "Anyone would have done the same if they'd entertained a harebrained idea and impulse to partner up with *her*."

"What went wrong?"

Roxana pulled off another eye-roll so exaggerated I wondered if she had an optician on speed dial. I pegged her to be about my age, in her thirties or forties, but her mannerisms were juvenile. She had Ella beat on the annoyed front.

"What went right, more like," she quipped wryly. "She only had ideas, no plans. She made excuse after excuse that she didn't have the spare cash to front me for a new camera, a new lens."

"Why'd you need new gear?" I shrugged. "Heck, you could even use a phone camera now, they're so good."

"Because it was a smart thing to do! Proper tools for a proper job."

I raised my hands at her outburst.

"You wouldn't understand. Photography is an *art*, not a little, simple hobby anyone can do with *smartphones*."

I held my tongue from further arguing about the aesthetic pros and cons of cameras and how they pertained to the theory of art. Countless influencers were making how much money via photos and videos captured on their phones? Plenty? I'd rest my case.

"A new camera and new lens would be business expenses," she stated, matter of fact.

"And since your 'business' never took off and crumbled before it began, you can't claim those expensive purchases anymore?"

She gaped at me, then took a threatening step toward me before seeming to think twice. "No." She grunted. "How dare you accuse me of that? You don't know me. And you don't know what you're talking about."

Hmm. Just like Jasper—worried about money.

"I did what anyone would have. Cut Yasmin loose." She glanced at the shed, then furrowed her brow at me. "In a figurative sense. I didn't kill her."

"Second time I've heard *that* one today."

"I didn't kill her," she insisted. "I cut her loose from the business. And it *is* going to happen, just I'll be doing it solo now, without her nagging and changing plans. Just like I figured it should be all along."

I crossed my arms and shifted my weight to my left leg. "All so you can still claim those expenses?"

"It's not just about the expenses!"

"Well, why'd you even team up with Yasmin in the first place? If you intended to do it as a solo endeavor?"

"Because I was doing all the work. I was fronting all the costs. She had some ideas, sure. She knew some people from cat shows and shelters."

I raised my brows. "Yasmin had connections, then?"

Roxana nodded. "As few as they were, yeah. But it seemed like a start. We'd do sample portrait services pro bono for shelters. To help them adopt out animals and to build a portfolio for our business. But, heck." She flapped her arm out to the side. "I could have approached them on my own. Anyone could."

"Probably."

"But it was Yasmin who first thought of it. She joined photography groups online. She applied for the journalist spot for Fayette's page too, to be the official photographer to upload pictures for the city page." She snorted a rude laugh. "Some photographer she was. She just liked to 'document' grievances. Anything she thought was wrong, she'd snap a picture and complain about them online.

"She saw that we were mutual friends in a couple of photog groups, and she reached out to *me* about this pet portrait idea." She shrugged. "At the time, I figured why not? I thought I could overlook her annoying habits and whiny attitude, but I never thought she'd just screw me over, having to pay for everything!"

"Mom?" Ella called from the back door to Barbara and Ingrid's house. "Is that you?" She'd paused in carrying out a bag of trash.

What a shock that was. These women were, gasp, expecting her to carry out a chore? And she was doing it?

"Yeah. Go on in. I'll be inside in a sec," I called back.

Then Ella proved she wasn't changing too much too soon. She disobeyed what I said and came to stand next to me, hugging herself in her hoodie.

"What's the wannabe photographer doing out here?" she asked bluntly.

Roxana dropped her mouth open. "Wannabe?" she screeched. "That was Yasmin." She pointed at the shed. "Yasmin was the wannabe."

Ella shrugged in that flippant way teenagers did. "Whatever. Why are you out here?"

Yeah. I crossed my arms and raised my brows at her.

"I was looking for something," Roxana sassed.

"At a crime scene," Ella said, deadpan. "Dumb."

"I have every right to look for what is mine." Roxana crossed her arms now, anteing up to Ella and my defensive pose.

I leaned forward, emphasizing my words like I was talking to a toddler. "Not on my property, you don't."

"What are you looking for?" Ella followed up. Then she smiled, saccharine sweet. "That way if we find it, we can let you know, hmmm?"

"Or finder's keepers," I added.

Roxana glowered at me. "Never mind," she huffed, turning to stalk away toward the alley. "Screw you!"

"Stay off my property!" I yelled as she strode away.

She stomped her foot as she stopped and spun to face us. "I wasn't on your property yet!"

"But you're on mine, and I'd like you off it, *now*," Ingrid said smugly, standing at the back door.

Roxana groaned, cursing some more as she turned back to skulk down the alley.

Ingrid put her fingers in her mouth and whistled sharply. "By the way," she hollered.

Roxana was nearly through the shrubs, but she turned again, glaring at Ingrid.

"If you were snooping and hoping to find a certain receipt that happened to fly over from next door"— she waved a slim piece of paper in her hand—"think again!"

AUBREY ELLE

Chapter Seventeen

The light was dim as the sun set, but I didn't miss how the color drained from Roxana's face.

What could be so bad, so incriminating, that she freaked out at Ingrid finding a receipt?

"Come on, Mom," Ella said as she tugged my coat sleeve. She glanced at Roxana as the woman fumed, turning on her heel to run away. "We found something!"

I see that.

Ingrid stood smiling at us as we climbed the steps to the back door. "I've had an eventful afternoon, too," I said.

"Oh?" Ingrid raised her brows, slipping Roxana's receipt into her pocket as she shut and locked the door after us.

I hadn't entered the house this way, but from the empty ceramic pots and assorted hand-held gardening tools on shelves, I gathered this might be a seasonal porch for the ladies.

"Yeah," Ella echoed. "Oh?"

"Yes. An eventful afternoon," I repeated as we entered the kitchen.

Barbara stood at the stove, stirring a pot. She perked at my arrival. "An eventful afternoon? Of course, you did. What'd ya think of Mr. Quinn, hmm?" A wink told me enough.

"Barbara," I warned. "Did you arrange for me to meet him for any other purpose than a job?"

"Who, me?" She feigned shock, placing a hand on her chest.

"Heaven help us," Ingrid muttered. "You do *not* want Barbara playing cupid for you."

"Hey!" She frowned at her best friend. "That's not true."

"Never mind, never mind that." Ingrid waved her off as she went to the counter where Ella was waiting for her. A blob of dough sat on a flour-coated tray.

"Well, wasn't he easy on the eyes?" Barbara asked.

"His looks didn't even cross my mind," I lied.

Ella scoffed. "You're not *blind*, Mom. It's okay to look."

Not yet, it isn't.

"Oh, he's adorable," Ingrid muttered. "We'd all be liars if we said otherwise. Let her go at her own pace. Naomi will know when she wants to consider another man in her life."

I nodded.

"That's not all," Barbara insisted. "He's so nice and funny and just so carefree. I thought you could use a happy-go-lucky kind of friend like that."

"Seeing as he hired me, he wouldn't be my friend. He'd be my boss."

"Yay! Congrats! But can't he be both?" Barbara asked, still stirring.

I shrugged. "That wasn't the eventful part, though."

"Getting a job after stressing about it for so long isn't *eventful*?" Ella asked.

"Well, it is."

"Then what's the *juicy* part you really mean?" Ingrid said.

I filled them in on Jasper and Melissa in the café. How she yelled at him, what she said, and then Jasper faking a faint.

"Because he's always the victim." Barbara rolled her eyes. "That man has yet to take blame for anything that goes wrong in life. I bet he was humiliated after

AUBREY ELLE

Melissa shouted at him like that, and he wanted people to feel sorry for him instead of thinking it was his fault for anything that could have displeased the local self-proclaimed pampered princess, AKA Melissa Varga."

Ella frowned, huffing a breath up to free her hair from her eyes as she kneaded dough. "Melissa who? Varga?"

"Yeah." Ingrid kneaded dough next to her. "She won the lotto a few years ago and since then, she's considered herself above everyone else in Fayette."

"Is she related to Mark Varga?" Ella asked. "Boyfriend to alleged cheerleader captain Bree Krogen?"

"Uh-huh," Barbara said, pointing at her. "You catch on quick to who's who."

Ella shrugged one shoulder, her hands still in the dough. "When everyone shares everything online, I'm quick to make connections."

I carried on, sipping water as I fell into my role of chopping veggies for a salad to accompany the lasagna. They were a rapt audience as I gave them a play-by-play of what Chief Mooney and Officer Donn said in line.

"And that's why Roxana was probably stressed about finding this receipt," Ingrid said. The dough was done, rolled out and ready to be layered in the pan. Barbara transferred the tomato-less sauce with meat, and Ella helped to layer the lasagna.

148

Ingrid joined me at the counter, showing me a receipt signed by Roxana. It was evidence of the woman purchasing a set of knives from the commercial bakery.

"Adam, the coroner, remember?" Barbara said as I skimmed the receipt. "Ingrid's former beau."

Ingrid laughed. "Beau? We just dated a couple of times. Anyway, I ran into him while I was at the grocery store. He's never been as uppity and closed-lipped about case details like her cousin," she said, smiling at Barbara. "He confirmed that Yasmin died from a stabbing, and the knife was still there. Tucked under her body, I guess. They confirmed it was one of a set of those knives that the bakery sells." She gestured with her fingers, to "draw" the picture. "It was quite cute, actually. They had the handles shaped like loaves of bread, but caricatures. They sell them seasonally as a little novelty, and the one used to kill Yasmin was from their Halloween series. The loaves of bread on the handles were dressed in costumes and such. Cute like gimmicky things."

"It sounds like Roxana showed up at the station, asking for what Yasmin could have had in her pockets," Barbara reminded us.

"And this receipt, that proves Roxana purchased the same said knives, was likely from her pocket," Ingrid said.

"Then why wasn't it still in her pocket when they took the body?"

"Did you forget about Georgie backing up and bumping into the shed?" Barbara asked me.

I had, actually.

"When he did, the doors to the van opened. The gurney wasn't locked in place"—Ingrid rolled her eyes—"and Adam says her body kind of slid off, almost flopping out to the ground."

Finished with the salad, I covered my face, trying not to laugh.

"Like National Lampoon's," Ella joked.

"And he guesses the paper might have slipped out and blown off," Ingrid added.

It had been so windy. That wasn't hard to believe.

"I found it when I started up my car earlier. I took it to the station and they confirmed it was evidence."

Frowning, I looked at the receipt before peering at Ingrid. "Then how's it *here* too?"

"I thought we should make a copy of it," Ella said.

"What, as a memento?" I asked.

"In case Roxana came snooping for it again," Ella said with her signature *duh* tone. "So she knows it's already found and reported. Then maybe she'll stop snooping."

"All right. Roxana has the motive," I said.

Barbara chimed in. "Because she hated Yasmin.

"She had the means," I said next.

"Because she bought that knife set," Ella filled in.

"But what about opportunity?" I asked. "The chief said she had an alibi."

"That was what I asked too. Adam says her roommate claimed Roxana was at home with her," Ingrid said.

"And that roommate's word is trusted?" I asked.

"Melissa Varga?" Barbara shrugged. "Who knows? I'd say it's kind of fishy. If you ask me, Melissa's sort of tied into this as well. She's the lover Jasper left Yasmin for."

I shook my head. "That was in the past, though, right? They *did* divorce, and he moved on, seeing Melissa."

"What motive would Melissa have to kill Yasmin?" Ella asked. "She already got her man."

"That means Melissa and Roxana's alibis are the same, each claiming the other was at home," Ingrid added.

"Let me get this straight," I said, waving my hands as though to clear the air. "Melissa Varga is Roxana's roomie?"

Ingrid took the pan and slid it into the oven while Barbara set a cooking timer. "It's a nice place, too," Barbara said.

"After winning the lotto, I imagine she'd splurge on a nice place," Ella said.

"Really big. Fancy loft in the historic end of town. I think the founder's house, actually," Ingrid said. "It was renovated years ago, and she snapped it up."

"And Roxana is her roommate," I repeated. "As in the woman I ran into in your backyard just now." I jerked a thumb to indicate the area of that confrontation. "As in the woman who seemed *super* worried about business expenses and the financial demands of starting a business."

Ella took a seat, picking up her phone to scroll. "Maybe Roxana got more than a place to rent from Melissa then, if she was so loaded."

Or not. Because that woman had practically screamed *I'm worried about money, please, life, don't make this any harder.* I sure hoped I didn't appear that desperate, but Roxana had *not* given me the impression she was financially comfortable. I wasn't sure I'd believe Melissa Varga was giving Roxana anything other than a spare room.

But could that mean Roxana would go so far as to kill the business partner who'd screwed her over with investments that had yet to earn back a penny?

Chapter Eighteen

While we waited for the lasagna to cook, we sipped tea and, well, spilled the tea. Barbara and Ingrid mostly bantered back and forth, teasing each other and me. If we weren't making jokes about how outlandish our speculations were, we were dissecting this murder case like we knew what we were talking about. Barbara and Ingrid might have known what they were talking about, clearly experts about who was who in town, but I offered a balance of *wait a minute* pauses of logic, shutting down angles of *what-if*s that just didn't seem likely.

Ingrid was liking Jasper as the murderer.

Barbara leaned toward Roxana.

I wasn't sure, and I refused to dismiss how cold Alexa had been about her sister. If she hadn't killed her, I'd be shocked.

We'd moved from tea to wine, too. Meanwhile, Ella left us, stepping up to handle Blane.

He'd called and texted throughout the day, and simply put, I still didn't have the patience for him.

When my phone buzzed on the table, I groaned. Ella spotted his name on caller ID and grabbed the device. "Oh, I'll talk to him and shut him up for a while."

I doubt anyone can truly shut him up. That man loved to hear himself talk. I wasn't sure Ella hated her father, but she clearly favored me, and I was fine with her trying to settle him down.

As she paced in the living room, I caught snippets of her conversation. Her blunt and flippant comments that, yes, the police were investigating why a dead body was on our property. Her repeated claims that no, said police weren't hillbillies, and yes, they seemed competent to do their jobs. No, we weren't in danger.

When she'd described the house, I smiled, hearing her lavish praise, exaggerating our new home so much it could have sounded like she was rating it five stars, comparable to a posh, spacious, turnkey palace. She said was "warm and cozy", not superheated from a faulty furnace.

And when she'd answered yes, I had found a job already, she'd been effusive there, too, stating I "passed a rigorous and taxing application process" to obtain an "executive academic administrator" position.

"If she's not a lawyer," Ingrid said of Ella, catching bits of her phone call as we set out plates for dinner, "that'll be a waste of talent."

I winced. I'd had enough of lawyers from my divorce. So much so that I never wanted to deal with one ever again. "I don't know. I'd want her to strive for something less…cut-throat and depressing."

Barbara chugged the last of her pre-dinner wine. "She can be a walking thesaurus then. She could hit gold on *Jeopardy* with that brainiac noggin of hers." She gasped, raising a finger. "She could write crossword puzzles."

"And fail to share her gift of arguing?" I teased, then shrugged. "Whatever her goals are, I'll support them."

"What about *your* goals?" Ingrid asked. "You always wanted to be an 'executive academic administrator'?"

I filled them in about why I'd never really had a job. Blane hadn't wanted me to work so as not to sully his family name. As I told them about my lack of work other than being a stay-at-home mom for Ella—which basically meant I lacked a chance to be *anything* else for a sense of self-purpose—I realized how much control he'd lorded over me. I loved raising Ella and being there for her. Being a mother was probably the one job I'd be most proud of. But it wasn't a crime to want something for myself, a career or purpose to work toward for myself.

My goals? Other than wanting to try to run again—missing that endorphin rush from my high school cross country days—I wasn't sure what else to put on a long-term to-do list.

"I'm sure Paul will be great to work with. Work for," I corrected. "But I don't know if it's a permanent job for me. I think I'm open to whatever the future has to offer." *Except dead bodies in my shed.*

"I know," Barbara said in that gasping, light-bulb-moment tone of sudden excitement. "You can help us open our Tea Time café and bakery!"

Ingrid groaned. "But I'm not done enjoying my retirement yet."

Ella returned to the kitchen as Ingrid set the lasagna on the table. "Well, that took longer than I'd hoped," my daughter complained. "He'd been calling me all day, and I hadn't wanted to listen to him. But I knew he wouldn't stop, so may as well get it over with. You're welcome, Mom. Your turn next time." She put my phone on the counter, then went to wash her hands at the sink. It seemed so domestic, so automatic. Her comment too, sharing something about her father. Ella had well and truly acclimated Barbara and Ingrid into her life, and what was more, she felt comfortable sharing her honest thoughts instead of bottling them up and being quiet and moody. Even if her thoughts were complaints about Blane. Her acceptance of our neighbors relaxed me, knowing she wouldn't begrudge me so much about moving us to Fayette.

"Because I had an idea," she said as she sat across from me.

"Only one?" I teased.

"For now. To start with." She waited until we all had a generous serving of the tomato-less lasagna before digging in.

It was so creamy, cheesier than a typical lasagna, and rich with minimal spices. Maybe too salty? But that could be the mozzarella.

"We're missing a critical clue to this case," Ella said, sounding much older than her almost seventeen years.

"And what's that?" Ingrid asked, passing a plate of garlic bread around.

Ella wiped her mouth before speaking. "We're trying to figure out who killed Yasmin and dumped her in the shed—"

Barbara interrupted. "Assuming it's only one person who did both." She waggled her brows, playing devil's advocate.

Ella seemed stumped, silent and frowning like she was disappointed in herself that she hadn't gone down that train of thought. "Assuming it is one person, then. Instead of figuring out *who* killed her, why don't we try to figure out *where?*"

I frowned, swallowing my mouthful before answering. "What would that do?"

"Because where she was killed should lead to clues about who would have been there to kill her."

I saw the sense in that, but did she actually hope one of us would have a strategy of how to determine where Yasmin was before she'd been left in the shed? What, combing through all of Fayette for a crime scene?

"I see what you mean," Ingrid said, nodding.

"So, where could she have been killed?" Ella asked.

"Your guess is as good as mine!" Barbara said, chuckling. "That feels like a needle-in-a-haystack approach."

"Okay, well, where did Yasmin go?" Ella asked. "Where did she work? Where did she like to spend time?"

Ingrid set her fork and napkin down, sighing. It didn't seem like a show of irritation of having to pause from eating, but more one of her thinking hard and figuring out the best answer.

I was grateful I could dig in and not have to speak.

"She was a medical coder," Barbara said, covering her mouth as she spoke with food she hadn't swallowed yet. "Right?"

"Yes. She worked at home, coding bills. I think that was how she got Jasper into his job, in insurance." She shrugged.

"She was a homebody, then?" Ella asked.

Ingrid shook her head. "No, not really. Remember, she wanted to make everyone's business *her* business."

And perhaps she stuck her nose where it didn't belong?

"She'd walk her cats—"

I gaped at Ingrid. "On a leash?"

"It's more common than you think, Mom," Ella chastised.

"She'd walk her cats on leashes, sometimes walk without them too. She'd attend council meetings, library information hours. She liked to be involved in the sense she wanted to be informed," Ingrid said. "Wouldn't you say?" She directed that question to Barbara.

"Hmm-mmm." She wiped her mouth. "When she and Roxana first mentioned their pet portrait idea, I think they met up at the café downtown. I saw them there, chatting with a laptop open."

"Why not at one of their homes?" I asked.

"I bet Yasmin didn't want someone at her house and bothering her cats on their turf," Ingrid said.

"And I would imagine Roxana knew better than to invite Yasmin to the apartment she shared with the lover Jasper left Yasmin for," Barbara added.

That added up. A public and neutral place to discuss the failure of a business endeavor that never took off.

"She took her cats to the vet, of course," Ingrid said. "And stopped at the grocery store often for a specific brand of cat food she requested to be ordered for her. Oh, and the county shelter, she would take stray cats there if she found them in town."

"In other words, no obvious place that would link her to one person, any one particular person who could have killed her," Ella said.

I got stuck on the idea of her cats. "What happened to them, anyway? Her cats."

Ella pulled her phone from her hoodie pocket and unlocked it. "Good question."

We ate as she scrolled until she huffed in surprise. "Wow. Listen to this. Actually, just read it. I don't want this to get cold."

She turned the phone around so the rest of us could lean in and read the post she had on the small screen.

When he's a ten but he drops what he's doing and takes in his former wife's pets. Knowing his current girlfriend (ME!) is HIGHLY allergic. WTH!

Melissa's ID showed as the poster. "So Jasper took her cats in?" I summed up. I read on though. A reply from some woman read: *Melissa, we had two cats when you were little. Since when are you allergic?*

I giggled at Melissa's mother calling her out on the lie.

Melissa's reply was awkward, too.

That's beside the point! It just proves he really can't let her go!

A few other commenters had replied, too. A shelter offering to take the cats. Another organization suggesting to have the cats spayed or neutered. Yet another, likely an organic pet food supplier, sharing a link to a coupon for treats.

"That was…kind of him," Barbara said.

"Especially since Jasper sounds like a dog lover and a lot of their conflict came from Yasmin preferring cats," Ella said.

Ingrid wore a pensive smirk on her face. "That crosses him off my suspect list then."

I scoffed. "Why?"

"If he didn't hate her enough to let her cats be abandoned after her death, I can't see him hating her enough to kill her either."

AUBREY ELLE

Chapter Nineteen

"Or maybe he took them in to throw *off* suspicion," Barbara challenged. "Just playing devil's advocate."

"No." Ingrid shook her head. "I can't see it."

We finished dinner tossing more ideas around, and as Barbara, Ingrid, and I had nearly finished off the bottle of wine, I was too settled to consider walking over to my house.

Ella wasn't eager to leave either. "It'll be so hot. Too hot to sleep there," she'd argued after we cleaned up the dishes together.

We'd carried on a steady conversation all evening, I hadn't even thought about the furnace until Barbara suggested we stay the night again. Gin—the furnace repairman—has returned the call earlier, saying he'd come the next day.

"If it's all right…" I said, still clinging to a worry that Ella and I were overstaying.

Ingrid laughed, swatting me on the arm. "Oh, stop that formal nonsense. I know you're only saying that to be polite." She winked. "You want to stay, too."

I grinned.

"Good," Ella said. "Because Barbara bet me she could beat me at Trivial Pursuit on the TV."

I rolled my eyes, wiping my hands on a dish towel. "Oh, boy. We're in for it now."

We settled in the living room where Ingrid and Ella quickly maintained a tie. Barbara folded quickly, as did I, and we sipped on the rest of the wine and chatted.

She told me more about their lives. Barbara had retired from being a museum curator. She'd married young, but it was clear they were a bad match when her ex decided in an early mid-life crisis moment that he wanted to be a monk and thus left her and moved.

"Oh, it suits him well," Barbara said cheerily. "He still sends postcards."

Children weren't an option for her due to an infertility issue, and she'd started a love of tea when Ingrid suggested it as an alternative to coffee, which was a trigger for her reflux. Also why we avoided the tomatoes in the lasagna.

She told us a little more about Ingrid, too, as she concentrated on beating Ella. Ingrid had gone into the service as a nurse, which was where she met and divorced her husband while stationed overseas in London—where she'd picked up her love of tea. Her ex passed away in action well after Ingrid had returned to the States, where she worked until retirement as an office gal at the water treatment plant—too tired of lousy patients and lousier bosses to stick to nursing.

It was nice to learn more about these two best friends, not only to lose the stranger label between us but also because it distracted me for a while from the sleuthing we'd all taken up with Yasmin's murder.

Until bedtime.

Ella was out as soon as her head hit the pillow in the guestroom, likely dreaming about her triumph of beating Ingrid at the game. A trick question about a Disney movie was how she'd bested the older woman.

Me? I was wide awake, too occupied with thoughts.

Again, I tried my tiring-out-eyes routine, scrolling on my phone. While I had the downtime to check back on everything I'd dismissed all day, I was even more awake, annoyed at the content of many of Blane's texts.

Why aren't you answering me?
Why won't you answer my calls?
Hello?

I heard you found a CORPSE at that house you're making Ella live in.

Hello?

Naomi, this is uncalled for and rude. I deserve better.

"Oh, you deserve better when you harass me all day long?" I whispered to myself.

Naomi, this isn't right. A dead body???!!! What is going on?

Is Ella okay? Is she traumatized?

HELLO?

If you don't answer, I'm calling my lawyer. This is unacceptable.

I sneered at my phone, doing my best mockery of what he likely looked like as he'd texted.

You cannot move my daughter to some lame town that has dead bodies lying around.

If you don't answer me, I'll call the "cops" there.

It's really childish of you to not answer your phone!

I cannot allow my daughter to live in an unsafe place.

I'm calling my lawyer and having custody revoked.

I narrowed my eyes, opening my text box to reply.

I have custody, and the judge isn't going to listen to whatever you claim. Ella is safe. Ella is fine. And she is happy. The person was left on the property before we moved here, and it has no connection to me or Ella or the house being habitable. Stop harassing me and pay attention to your new family.

I should have put my phone down, but that man irritated me so much, I wasn't at all sleepy now. Determined to focus on something else, I scrolled through the social media for Fayette again, trying to justify how quickly I'd defended living here with Ella.

Obviously a dead body wasn't an ideal welcome gift, but I wasn't subjecting Ella to danger. Or unsafe living conditions.

Am I?

Technically, we hadn't *lived* in our house yet, staying for the second night with Barbara and Ingrid.

I shook my head. No. I was handling this as I should. Chief Mooney stressed that Ella and I could move in. And since we never knew Yasmin and could therefore have no connection with her or any reason for her murder, what happened to her couldn't be associated with us.

Blane knew how to strike where it hurt, though. He admitted he fought for custody *just because*, not because he wanted to be a father to Ella. Her statements to the judge were what really finalized it.

Ella in no shape or form expressed a desire to live with her father.

But that didn't mean Blane couldn't raise a fit and claim I was unfit to be a mother and overrule Ella's input.

I'm fit. I'm not an unfit mother. But the quicker we had closure on Yasmin's murder—to once and for all prove her death didn't pose a risk for Ella and me to live here—Blane's threat would hang over my head.

How dare he make it sound like I'm dragging her to a hotbed of crime and danger.

Fayette, from what I'd experienced so far, was likely a lovely little town. Winter made everything look and feel drab, but come spring, I bet this small area would blossom and be a wonderful place to raise Ella.

Crime seemed low— notwithstanding Yasmin's murder, of course.

I skimmed the posts online again, looking for signs that crime and malice were the norm. Now hyperware of Blane's harsh texts, I ignored how Yasmin had commented on most of the things pertaining to people misbehaving. Ingrid and Barbara had already explained she liked to consider herself the neighborhood watch queen and wasn't shy about tattling and complaining.

"Maybe someone just wanted to silence her for always complaining," I mumbled to myself.

Even still, I wasn't subjecting Ella to some horrible, perilous slum.

There were a few reports of package thefts—*which can happen anywhere, especially around the holidays.*

Several complaints were shared about needing speed bumps in a certain neighborhood by the library—*a valid concern that can apply in any town with reckless drivers.*

Then the usual calling out of people not picking up dog poop on the sidewalk. *Again, a minor issue that's not endemic to Fayette.*

Fayette wasn't a horrible place to raise my daughter. I was sure of it.

But I bet that would sound more convincing once Yasmin's murder was solved and left to be old news.

AUBREY ELLE

Chapter Twenty

I woke in the morning cranky and tired from lousy sleep. Ingrid had already left for an early-morning aquatics class, so it was Barbara who offered me a cup of Earl Grey to boost-start my day.

"Is Ella as much of a ray of sunshine as you are?" she asked, sitting with me at the kitchen table.

I frowned. "I'm not a grump."

She smiled. "Oh, I was teasing. Not a good night's rest?"

I shook my head. "Never is."

"Maybe some exercise will help?"

I slanted my brows at her as I sipped my tea. I wasn't a morning grouch like Ella, but did anyone want to face such personal criticism first thing just after dawn?

"I slept like a log last night."

Again, I deadpanned at her. "Rub it in, why don't ya."

She giggled. "Oh, you're so cute. I think I slept better than usual because I was so active and busy helping Ella empty the moving van."

I set my mug down. "Oh, no." *She overdid it.* "I'm sorry. I didn't expect you to wear yourself out and—"

"But I did." She tilted her head. "In a good way. Which is why I think I slept so well."

"Oh." I sat back in the chair, relieved I hadn't broken her.

"Ingrid swims. We both walk. In the summer, we garden." She paused to sip her tea. "I also sign up for kickboxing. We have a little weight room in the basement, but the stationary bike does squeak if you go too fast, and the weights aren't taxing enough anymore."

"Please, put little old out-of-shape me to shame."

"How about we show you the health club that started up downtown someday?"

I shrugged. "I have thought about trying to run again."

She beamed. "Ingrid loves to jog."

"Jeez. Does Fayette have a fountain of youth or something?"

Patting my hand, she sagely said, "Our only secret is if you don't use it—"

"You lose it," I finished for her. "I'll think on it." Yawning, I stretched and checked the time. "When is Gin supposed to show up?"

She glanced at the black kitty-cat clock swishing its tail. "A couple hours."

"Maybe I can sort out some things in the house. Move around with your suggestion to tire myself."

"So long as you don't overheat!"

"Ella won't like it but—"

"Why doesn't she sleep in then? I can send her over when she's up. Her winter break is nearly over, isn't it? Then she'll be up before dawn."

"And hating it. You don't mind?"

She shrugged. "What's there to mind? I've got this pot to empty and I haven't even started my crossword yet. She can sleep in and wake when she wants."

"Thank you, Barbara," I said, squeezing her hand. "You're a godsend."

She huffed a laugh. "And here I thought I was better at being devil's advocate."

I had only been in the house for an hour, unboxing books and sorting them on bookshelves, when Barbara texted that Gin would come even earlier. He was there even sooner than that, grinning and cheery in overalls and a toolbox in hand. "Morning!" he greeted when I opened the front door.

"Hi, Gin. I'm Naomi," I said, stepping back to let him in.

"Whew." He stuck his tongue out and fanned himself. "Babs wasn't kidding when she said this place was sweltering!"

"Babs?" I couldn't help but laugh at his nickname.

"Oh, it's an old joke. Back from high school." He leaned in for a stage whisper, as though she could hear him. "Don't tell her I said it," he teased with a wink.

I showed him to the basement, and he set his toolbox down as he surveyed the furnace. "I remember installing this for Fred. It's got, oh, I bet at least another couple years on it yet."

Oh, good. I could postpone replacing it for a while then.

"And I bet it won't take much to get her back to normal now."

I smiled, kind of amused at him dubbing a furnace a *she*, kind of like how sailors dubbed boats a feminine name. He went on to explain the parts and mechanisms he thought were malfunctioning. It would take a few hours to get the parts, but he could tweak it so it would stop at a slightly lower temperature until he returned later before dinnertime.

"We've been staying at Barbara and Ingrid's house since we arrived and realized the heat wasn't working correctly," I said.

"They are such sweethearts. Ballbusters, but sweet."

"I'm sure they wouldn't mind us for another night if need be." I watched him tinker, mildly curious. Not so much about the furnace but more so about the fact he knew my neighbors so well. The stories he could share... I imagined there were many. "My daughter sure seems to enjoy their company."

"I heard you got a teenager," he said. "Barbara sounds like she's already adopted her! You've been here, what, a day or two and she's already acting like your girl is her unofficial grandkid."

I smiled.

"Besides, no one would blame you for hesitating to live here just yet. What, with Yasmin in your shed..."

I sighed. "That too." Reminded of my conviction last night, I spoke up firmly. "But I'm sure that case will be closed soon, and when it is, this will just be another family home, not a crime scene."

"Oh, sure, sure. Mooney might look like he's tired and burned out, but that's because he's busy off the clock as grandpa. He's a sharp one. Top of the class when he was the class geek and all. I trust him to figure it out," Gin said with a nod. "But her murder—that case—sure is all everyone's been talking about."

Me included.

"What people might not realize…" he said, leaning in and making a show of checking that no one was eavesdropping despite it being just the two of us down here. He tapped the side of his head. "I hear them all."

I narrowed my eyes, nodding just to seem like I agreed and was not suspicious. *Like…voices in your head?*

"When I'm on calls, in people's homes…" He chuckled, returning to tinker with a panel on the furnace. "People don't realize how clearly sound travels to the basement. Ducts, pipes, crawl space. I hear lots."

I laughed. "Well then. I'll consider myself warned and not spill state secrets when you come by."

He had a good laugh too, and he launched back into a summary of what he could do to the furnace for now. It wasn't much, since he had to wait on the parts, but he offered to do a little inspection while he was here. That was how we ended up almost touring the house.

"Just be happy Fred updated this place from the radiators. That boiler was ancient," Gin said wiping sweat from his brow as we climbed the stairs.

"Are they harder to maintain?" I asked.

"Yes and no. Now the ones at the historical building downtown?" He exhaled a sound of dread. "There are *three* of them in there. Three!"

I waited at the front door as he zipped up his tool kit. "That's where Melissa and Roxana share an apartment, huh?"

"For now," he said, a sly glint in his eye.

"Why for now?" I asked as I opened the front door to let in some fresh, cooler air. Windows were cracked as far as they could be, but the door allowed a good breeze of chilliness to sneak in.

"Well, I've been there often. Every winter, those boilers act up. It'd be a headache to replace them, and an even bigger headache to install ducts, I don't think the owners will ever want to convert it all. So…since I've been there a lot lately, I hear them arguing and such."

"Melissa wants to kick Roxana out?" I guessed.

"No, not quite. But Roxana seems to feel threatened, like she'll be forced out." He dabbed his forehead with a hanky, then pushed it back in his uniform coveralls. "Jasper's been begging Melissa to move in with him for so long now. I've heard him visiting too, asking her why, why, why."

"I heard she stalled because she wanted Yasmin to remove things she'd never taken from his house after the divorce was done."

Gin nodded, smiling mischievously. "True. True. But I heard that girl flat-out say she just hated the idea of having dogs. Too smelly. They licked her too much.

She never told *him* that, but she'd gripe to Roxana after he left."

And claim she was allergic as an excuse, it seems.

"But it sounded like Yasmin finally picked up whatever things she'd stalled to collect. Jasper was pressing his case more and more, and from what I heard, it kind of sounded like Melissa was going to move in."

He watched me, almost smiling, one brow raised. Like he was waiting for me to find a punchline.

"Okay…"

"If Melissa moved in with Jasper, she'd be out of a home. Mooching off Melissa…" He shrugged. "Roxana would never be able to afford that luxury apartment on her own!"

"Is that so?" I said, considering this information.

I had already come to the conclusion that Roxana was sensitive about money, perhaps needy for it. Stingy, even. But if that was the case, wouldn't she have wanted Yasmin alive, not dead, since the reminder of Yasmin at Jasper's house prevented Melissa from wanting to move in—which would force Roxana out of her current residence?

Chapter Twenty-One

"Anyhow," Gin said as I mused about what he'd heard at that building. "Babs says you're also looking for a car, huh?"

"I am." I pointed at the moving van I'd rented. I needed to return that today before I had a crazy bill as it sat there.

"My nephew's got one he's trying to sell. He just moved to college, and he's thinking he'll stick around for summer classes and such, too."

"That's convenient. I worried Fayette might not have a big selection of used cars locally."

Gin nodded. "Yep. And it's a solid, reliable car. My brother always made sure he kept up on maintenance. If you like, you can ride along with me and I'll show you." He patted his pocket. "I've been carrying around a spare key. Since my brother works third shift at Wilson's Bakery and sleeps during the day."

"Really? You wouldn't mind?"

"Oh, not at all. I've got time before my next appointment."

I checked in with a text to Ella, but she didn't reply, so I figured she was still sleeping.

A call to Barbara confirmed my daughter was in the shower.

"That's right. Henry's hoping to sell his car. Why didn't I think of that?" she replied. "Go ahead. I bet Gin would sell it to you for a good price. A steal, really. I'll tell Ella that you'll be back shortly."

"Okay, Babs," I said, teasing her.

She groaned. "Ohhhh. That man. Never mind that nickname."

"Yes, ma'am." I laughed, hanging up and wondering why she disliked the moniker so much.

Another story to ask for at another time. How quickly I'd come to anticipate spending time with her, too.

Gin drove into town, tossing out factoids about various houses and buildings, namely tricky jobs he'd done at various locations in Fayette. It sure seemed he was the local go-to man for HVAC concerns, and I was pleased he was personable, too. Not an in-and-out contractor who cared less about his clients.

"Hey, you mind if we stop at the historic building real quick?" he asked. "Now that we were talking about it, I wonder if that's where I left my phone charger." He lightly smacked the steering wheel in annoyance at himself. "Sometimes when I'm on a job in an empty, quiet house, I listen to podcasts and audiobooks on my phone."

"You mean when no one is there to talk for you to eavesdrop?" I teased.

He winked, grinning at me. "Yeah, pretty much. But it burns the battery so fast I sometimes have to charge it while I'm on a job. I've searched everywhere, and when I retrace my steps the last time I remember having that charger, it was in that basement, at the beginning of the week. Do you mind if we stop in real quick so I can look?" He glanced at me before paying attention to the road again. "You can even sit in the van if you want. I'll just look real quick."

"Sure. That's not a problem." I smiled, craning my neck to look through the windshield. "I haven't driven down this side of town yet. I'm kind of curious what this 'historic' founder's building looks like."

"Oh, it's neat. Architecturally and all."

"Just not so great with three temperamental boilers?"

He grunted a laugh. "You got that right."

Gin's assessment was accurate. Ornate scrollwork ran along the ledges that marked the stories, and the white-painted bricks gave it an old-timey design. New, modern windows gave it an updated look, but the gargoyles near the downspouts retained proof of its age.

"Sure stands out," I said, peering up at the three-storied building.

"That it does." Gin parked his work van near a door at the back, and since I didn't want to look like a stranger sitting in his vehicle, I decided I'd just head in with him. Besides, I didn't have a chance to say I'd do otherwise because he'd fallen into a steadfast ramble about the boilers. Part a history lesson, a gripe about the boilers operating in different areas of the building, and also a mechanical lecture on how boilers worked in old houses, he spoke without a pause as he led the way into the basement.

Once we set foot in the cellar space, his voice was drowned out by the humming boilers at work. "Hang on a second," he yelled to be heard over the boilers. "Light's right over here."

Some daylight shone behind me, from the stairwell leading to the basement, but it was pitch-dark further in.

Using the flashlight on his phone, he found his way to the wall.

I shifted my weight as I waited, wondering if the loudness of the boilers was normal or a sign of their temper.

I frowned, distracted by how my shoes kind of stuck *and* slipped as I fidgeted.

But when Gin turned the light on, I couldn't even think. Not about boilers, my shoes, or the age of this building. I was stunned, shocked silent at the blood all over the floor.

Gin sucked in a breath, holding out an arm to barricade me, as though something would pop out and attack.

As my gaze landed on a shiny form of metal, I knew nothing was waiting down here for us. The crime had already happened and passed.

A Y-shaped keychain glittered next to a squeezable cat stress toy strung to a set of keys.

Yasmin's keys.

We'd stumbled upon the crime scene.

Ella's logic from last night returned to me.

"Because where she was killed should lead to clues about who would have been there to kill her."

And in the basement of this historic founder's building, that was a very interesting clue to ponder.

Roxana?

Melissa?

Jasper, when he'd visited?

Does Alexa deliver mail here, too?

Gin cleared his throat. "I think...I think..." he stammered, shaken.

"I think it's time to call Chief Mooney," I finished for him.

Pale and wide-eyed, he faced me and nodded.

Chapter Twenty-Two

Officer Donn showed up first, then Chief Mooney. He did a double-take at me. "What are *you* doing here?"

Gin explained, but the chief still frowned at me while Donn was in the basement. "Please don't tell me you'll move here and have a knack for finding trouble…"

"I already have moved here," I pointed out.

He grunted. "As I well know. Since your husband—"

"*Ex*-husband," I corrected.

"—called to demand details of a case he has no business asking about."

I winced.

The chief's frown creased his brow more. "He wasn't abusive, was he?"

"No. Not like you're probably thinking. More a headache than anything else."

He patted my back. "Good you're free of him then." I was touched by his immediate concern, and I felt comforted that he'd seemed to just accept me as one of Fayette's. That he'd be a buffer between me and my past with Blane.

Switching to business at hand, he interviewed me, and then Gin. By the time other officers arrived, as well as the forensic team, Chief Mooney told Gin he was free to leave, to drop me off at home.

"You okay, there, Naomi?" Gin checked as he drove me home.

I nodded. "I...I think so." I licked my lips, searching for the best way to word it. "It wasn't as bad as finding her body. And knowing she'd been stabbed somewhere nearby...well..."

"Kind of expecting it?"

I cringed and glanced at him. "Is that bad?"

"Logical," he said with a grunt. "You sure are a cool one, kid. Levelheaded. No hysterics."

I shrugged. "I numb it off and try to be pragmatic." Rolling my head on the headrest, I sighed and looked at him. "You have yet to meet my daughter. She...keeps me on my toes. I guess she's made me hardy over the years."

"I can see why Barbara and Ingrid are so taken with you two," he said.

He dropped me off with a promise to return later that day when the part for my furnace came in. His nephew's car would still be there whenever I was ready to look at it.

"You have a nice, calming, relaxing lunch then," I told him, worried if he was still upset and bothered by finding that scene.

"Oh, I will. I will. It's like you said. We had to be expecting a bloody mess like that somewhere since we knew she was stabbed." He nodded, narrowing his eyes absently. "And now that they can investigate it, I hope Mooney and his crew get a clue." He turned his serious, tough gaze to me. "Because I'll rest easier once I know the killer's caught. I'm not a fan of knowing one of Fayette's own was killed in cold blood, no matter how much people complained about that, well, that complainer."

I agreed and said I'd see him later.

I didn't bother going to my house. Instead, I let myself in through Barbara's side door. Ella practically launched herself at me, hugging me tightly.

"I was chatting with Adam when he got the message from the chief," Ingrid said. "How gruesome."

"Mom! I can't believe you stumbled upon *two* crime scenes," Ella exclaimed, holding me at arm's length.

Because I'm an unfit parent? I mentally shook off that nagging worry put there by my ex. I wasn't unfit. I was just…well, unlucky of late.

"Technically, Gin found it. I only happened to be there with him," I said sheepishly.

As it was quickly becoming a habit, we took our seats at the square table in the kitchen, surrounded by their teacups and teapots. We'd already chosen "our" seats of the two Barbara and Ingrid didn't take. Like assigned placement at school, we had a spot that suited us.

"I'll make us a pot of English Lavender," Barbara said with a nod. "To help us relax from the news."

I filled them in, sharing what I could about the scene. It was pointless to speculate beyond the obvious. Yasmin's keys were a telltale clue she'd been there, and it wasn't like we could assume that scene was linked to any other stabbing victim of late. Yasmin was it.

"I still can't see Roxana killing her, though," Ingrid said.

Ella scoffed. "Because you still think it was Jasper?"

"What about Melissa?" I added.

"What would she gain from killing Yasmin?" Ingrid asked.

I shrugged. "I don't know. Jealous Yasmin had Jasper first? Some form of slight being the *other woman*?"

Barbara shook her head, tapping her finger on the table for attention to cut in. "It could have been anyone, really. That door wasn't locked, was it?" she asked me.

I thought back to when Gin and I arrived. He'd been yakking and yakking away, but now that I replayed it in my mind, I shook my head. "Gin didn't unlock it. Just pushed it open." I frowned at her. "How'd you know that?"

"Because Ms. Bellette, who works in the dry cleaning place next door, has seen the water meter man go in. He just walks in and walks out. No lock," she said. To further clarify, she tilted her head toward me and added, "We're in the same yoga class at the health club and she likes to gossip. She notices"—she snapped her fingers one way—"every"—snap to the other way—"thing."

"Like Yasmin did?" Ella asked.

Barbara shook her head. "Ms. Bellette concerns herself with what happens at her storefront. She's protective of the business since she started it up all on her own, with her own funds. Yasmin concerned herself with all of Fayette just for the sake of being nosy."

Big difference when you put it that way.

"So the door isn't secured, which means anyone could have happened by it and used that space to murder Yasmin," Ingrid summed up.

I raised my hand. "Question. Why would Yasmin be there?"

"To meet Roxana?" Barbara guessed. "To talk about the photo business."

"Nah. They seemed to have chosen the café to talk shop," Ingrid said. "Besides they split and parted ways from the partnership well before Christmas."

And on and on we debated and chatted. Ella left the kitchen, escaping to the quiet in the guestroom to study her move for her online chess game. Barbara started a batch of tea biscuits, and Ingrid tended to laundry in the basement.

I sat at the kitchen table, prompted to fill out the health coverage and miscellaneous forms Paul had given me yesterday at the café.

How was that only yesterday? Life was just blurring by since we'd arrived in Fayette. *Or maybe it's just the hectic circumstances we'd met upon arrival.*

He'd texted that he'd come to pick them up this afternoon, if that was all right with me.

Sure thing. But stop at Barbara and Ingrid's house. We're visiting.

Visiting? I almost laughed, scribbling my information on the forms. It sometimes felt like we'd moved in here.

A while later, a knock sounded on the door. Barbara answered it, leading Paul back to the kitchen where I rushed to finish the last of the forms.

"Sorry I had to rush you on those," he said, taking a seat but declining Barbara's offer for a cup of the tea.

"Oh, no worries," I said, glancing up only long enough to smile at him.

"I just want to make sure I get them scanned before I leave."

"Ah. Another marathon?" Barbara asked.

"No, just a ten-K."

"*Just* a ten-K," I teased.

"Naomi runs," Barbara said cheerily.

I glanced at her, lingering so she'd feel the laser effect of my deadpan. "I do not."

"You want to," Barbara insisted.

"I've *thought* about trying to take up running again," I corrected, my gaze back on the form. What did they need to know my BMI for? These were awfully invasive personnel forms.

"I could show you some beginner routes," Paul offered. "Fayette's not large enough for variety if you're a fan of long-distance, but I've figured out a decent attempt of including hills for an extra challenge."

I peered at him again, so touched by his offer. It sounded genuine, and I was excited he seemed so enthusiastic about the sport. I'd run for varsity way back when, and I couldn't help but feel a connection to his attitude about the activity other sports used as a punishment.

A fellow runner. Or, almost, if I tried to incorporate exercise into my life again. *He's sweet. Generous. Not bad on the eyes...*

I caught a glimpse of Barbara arching her back to lean in to my field of vision, standing behind Paul as she held a bowl and mixed it. Her smile was too smug and knowing, and I sighed, returning to the form.

Not the time to even consider that...

I cleared my throat, realizing I hadn't replied. "Thanks. Maybe I'll take you up on that one day."

"Uh," he said, glancing at Barbara, "speaking of running. I managed to squeeze in a five-miler earlier. Rick Donn usually runs with me, but he said he was dealing with a call."

I nodded, finished with the forms, and handed them over to him. "Yeah, I was there. Gin called it in. We found the spot where Yasmin had to have been stabbed."

Paul grimaced. "That's what Miss Bellette said, too. She was standing outside when I stopped by."

"You stop at the dry cleaner on your runs?" I asked.

"I didn't have my wallet on me when I picked up my shirts yesterday, and I promised I'd stop by on my run today and pay up."

Kind. True to his word... Again, I shook the thoughts of admiration from my mind.

"She said she wasn't surprised it could have happened there since no one really locks that door."

"What a security mistake that is," Barbara said.

He nodded. "I agree. But what she said was *really* suspicious was who she saw going in there lately. More than once. Someone who shouldn't have been there."

Barbara swatted his shoulder with a spatula she had yet to put in her batter. "Well, don't just sit there and keep us in suspense. Who was it?"

"Alexa. The mailwoman, Alexa Krogen. She saw her sneaking in through that basement door."

AUBREY ELLE

Chapter Twenty-Three

"I'll assume the mailboxes to the tenants in that building are *not* located in the basement," I said after Paul left.

As soon as he had, thanking me for filling out the forms in a rush, Barbara hollered for Ella and Ingrid to come in the kitchen so we could share the news about the case.

"No. I think the mailboxes are at the entrance the building where an apartment used to be but was in the process of being renovated," Ingrid said. "If you pass by the front of the building, you can see a little hallway leading in, with mail slots along the wall."

"No reason for Alexa to be near the basement, then, huh?" I asked.

"Not according to what I would guess, no," Ingrid said.

Barbara enlisted Ella into helping her make tea biscuits, and earlier, Ingrid said she just *had* to finish re-organizing the laundry room. She hadn't put the holiday decorations and tree things away yet because the storage space wasn't ideal.

"Gin should be back later," I said, watching Ella at the counter with Barbara. "Maybe it's cooled enough that we can sleep there tonight."

"But it'll smell," Ella said.

Is this a new obstacle she's throwing up for some hidden reason?

"I said I'd pick up her paint," Ingrid said.

"Oh." Ella's wish to have a non-clinical-white bedroom had escaped my notice. She had said that.

"Ingrid and I used an app yesterday, when we were moving things in. And I ordered it."

Ingrid winced. "You're not upset, are you?" She smirked at Ella. "I *told* you we should ask her before ordering it. You can't refund a custom order."

"Which I still think is a lame policy. What if you order, and it's just not right?"

"That's the small, fine print of the app that catches people, I guess," Ingrid said. "Hence why it is slightly cheaper to go through the app."

"No, no. It's fine." I had already planned to paint it sooner or later. "I just worry we've…well, moved in *here*, instead of next door. Cramping on your space."

"Bah," Barbara said. "The universe clearly wanted us to be best friends. A fab four of girl greatness. We're neighbors. We'll look out for each other."

"I really wouldn't want to sleep with paint fumes. But I would like us to be settled and somewhat closer to a routine. You know," I said, glancing at Ella. "Because you'll start school in four days, give or take."

She lifted a hand in a dismissive wave. "Like school is ever an issue for me."

Grades, no. Waking up on time without me nagging the world's grumpiest sleepyhead? Not so much.

"Then I'll grab the paint in a bit," Ingrid said. "I need to get some new anchors for that other shelving unit. Then you can paint tonight, let Gin do his work, and move in tomorrow."

It was a plan. "I'll try to sort out some more things and empty boxes," I said, checking my phone. "Besides, I think I'll have quite a few deliveries coming in."

"Your bed set?" Ella asked. "Because that's another reason I want to stay here again tonight." She smiled at Barbara. "If it's okay. Of course." Then she faced me, wincing. "Because as much as I love you and would share my bed with you, I don't *want* to. You move too much, tossing and turning."

"Oh, the love," I said wryly. But she was right. I wasn't a deep and relaxed sleeper.

"You girls are welcome anytime," Barbara said. "No, no, no. That's too thick," she scolded Ella.

"You said a quarter of an inch."

"Which isn't that. Roll it thinner, honey."

Ella sassed back. "Let's get a ruler. That *is* a quarter of an inch."

"Oh, you." Barbara sighed. "It's an approximation. I don't remember exactly what a quarter of an inch looks like. My eyes aren't as good as yours."

"Which probably means you shouldn't *eye*ball things?" Ella teased.

"Shush, you. Ah. There are my glasses." She snatched them from down the counter. "Oh. That's not a quarter of an inch."

I left to Barbara and Ella giggling and Ingrid checking her wallet was in her purse.

"You sure you're okay with us getting the paint without your approval?"

"It's fine." I glanced back, smiling at the pair in the kitchen. "I think it's just…letting go."

Ingrid gaped at me. "You mean…taking over Ella? And being too pushy and *right there* all the time?"

I smiled, taking to chance to cross a boundary and give her a side hug. "Letting go of constantly making sure Ella's not a nuisance. Or I am. Blane's family was just so…" I grimaced like I'd swallowed lemon juice. "It's a *good* adjustment, how you two are taking her under your wing. It's a different kind of role modeling I can't give her as her mom."

Ingrid nodded.

"It is different though. Letting go as in me getting used to knowing she *is* welcome and valued, not an obligation or responsibility. A good letting-go of being so high-strung to not make waves. Back in Swenton, her wanting to paint her room would be a huge deal, inviting criticism from her father, her 'grandma', her friends. Not to mention they'd never let her actually paint anything and risk making a mistake. Here, she can make a simple decision for herself without having to defend it or justify it. It's…it's a shock."

"You are both welcome," Ingrid promised outside.

She went to her car, and I headed to our house to put more things away.

When Gin knocked on the door, I had sweated through my t-shirt. I wiped my brow and stalled at the front door, relishing the noon air seeping in.

"Windows don't help?" he asked with a wince. "Sorry I couldn't fix it sooner."

"It's not your fault the part took a while." I felt sorry he had to be inconvenienced driving to another town to get the part as it was. "And no, the windows don't do much."

"Replacing them would be a handy investment," Gin commented as he headed to the basement. "If you're planning to stick around."

I smiled. "We are." I didn't tack on a *for now*, either.

Gin repaired the furnace shortly, and when it was only the fans on, not heat, I hoped relief would come soon. Maybe it'd be too hot to paint today—which was such irony as it was nearly January in a Midwest winter!

After he left, I set to clearing out the boxes I'd emptied in the kitchen. Operating on autopilot with nineties alt-rock playing on my phone, I'd made quick work of getting this home to look more lived in. Or at least more likely to be lived in.

Ella wasn't fighting me every step of the way.

We had the best neighbors on earth.

I had a job.

The idea of running again seemed possible, not a 'goal' I would have to defend against my ex's complaint it wasn't 'proper' to sweat so much in public.

And it couldn't be much longer until Chief Mooney solved the murder case that had at first plagued our move to Fayette with bad tones.

I felt good, on top of the world like things could be looking up.

So when my phone rang, and I saw it was Angela, my former mother-in-law, I felt ready to take her call and tell her to leave me alone. Confidence was a heady thing.

As I'd expected, she'd only called to berate me, to harass and nitpick, and to judge me for my choice to move Ella to Fayette. Her lack of concern about *me* was a given. She'd never cared for me, and her thoughts about Ella were not borne of love for her only grandchild, just a worry that any of her flesh and blood must be raised according to the exacting statutes that came with being a Front.

I refused to budge, letting what she said in one ear and out the other as I brought flattened boxes to the porch where I'd leave them for easier disposal come recycling day.

With my phone between my shoulder and my cheek, I multitasked clearing out the boxes, back and forth from the house to the porch.

When she railed about removing Ella from my custody, an arrangement she had no say in, as we both knew, my quota was exceeded.

"Listen, and listen, good, Angela, because I won't waste my breath repeating myself. Ella lives with *me*. As I've done since the day she was born, I will see to her safety and happiness. *Me*. I am her mother, and I will do what I think is right for her."

A delivery van approached, the employee raising his eyes at my shouting as he hurried up the steps to leave a box. I nodded thanks at him, not deterred from the phone call I was finishing.

"I moved her out of Swenton to escape your ugly, vile mouth and the hurtful, critical nonsense you spew. I don't care if you think our new home is embarrassing, or I'm pitiful to be a working mom. I don't care if you think it's a disgrace there happened to be a dead body in my shed. That I had nothing to do with."

Tunnel-visioned in telling her off, I hurried faster, venting my anger in nearly rushing the boxes outside in a need to burn off this energy and adrenaline that came from speaking to Angela.

"For the last time. Do not call me. Do not text me. You are not good enough to be in my daughter's life. You are not good enough to constantly judge my every action. I will always choose a way to see to her health and happiness before I concern myself with any pathetic worry I have about appeasing *you*."

I hung up, my finger jamming the icon to end the call, and I huffed, sagging in relief as I slumped against the house's exterior wall as I paused on the porch. Closing my eyes, I breathed in deeply.

There! I told her all right. Now she'd complain to Blane and then resume her calls and nasty texts in a week or so.

I should just change my number. If only the custody agreement would allow me to. I smirked, shaking my head.

"You tell her," someone said.

I jolted, not realizing I wasn't alone. Traffic was minimal on our street, but I hadn't heard another delivery vehicle pull up.

Angela Krogen stood a step below the porch, her light-blue uniform and the stack of small boxes in her arms indicating she was next in the line for deliveries today.

"Oh." I was confused that she wasn't acting so snooty with me. "Thanks?"

She jerked her thumb over her shoulder, and when I looked, I saw the postal van parked down the street, mostly hidden from my view unless I stepped into the front lawn.

"I heard you as I grabbed more from the van." She raised her brows, handing me my boxes. "Good on you. Telling her off."

I was too stunned to reply. Was she bipolar? Selective amnesia? Because the last time she was here, she'd been really standoffish and mean to me. Now she was...complimenting me?

"A momma's always going to do right for her daughter." She lifted her chin. "No one messes with my Bree either. Not if I can help it."

Ah. A mother-to-mother thing. I understood her attitude now. I'd gained respect for defending my daughter.

"My former mother-in-law," I said as an explanation. "Ella doesn't need that toxic influence anymore."

Alexa scoffed, as though saying *you're telling me*. "It's bizarre how bad 'family' can be sometimes."

I thought back to her comment in parting the last time I saw her, just yesterday. *Blood* is *blood*, she'd sassed back to Barbara. Like having relatives was a bad thing.

"You don't get along with your mother-in-law either?" I asked.

She shrugged. "Never met her."

Uh-oh. I didn't want to delve into that. It sounded like a long, bad story.

Reaching into her messenger bag, she collected a handful of my mail. Although when I took it, I realized it was mostly for Fred, not me.

Shoot. Return the van. Contact Gin to check out his nephew's car. And check in at the post office to update the address stuff.

A tree branch cracked and a twig fell down. Alexa started and sidestepped the landing.

And contact someone about that tree.

My to-do list was only growing by the instant, but with this woman standing in front of me, I shoved those tasks to the back of my mind and focused on her.

"Why are you looking at me like that?" Alexa asked, her face scrunching into a scowl, reminding me of the woman I'd met.

May as well come right out with it.

"Why were you in the basement of the historic founder's building?"

"For Pete's sake." She huffed, slapping her hand to the thigh that wasn't covered by the messenger bag. Swapping her gum to her other cheek, she sneered. "Where'd you hear that?"

I crossed my arms and shrugged. "The dry cleaning lady?" She groaned. "She sure blabbed fast. I heard some cats, all right?"

Cats?

"A couple weeks ago, I heard this meowing and crying. I hate the thought of an animal in pain. I worried something was stuck and hurt. So I poked around and saw some mama cat had managed to squeeze in through a busted window. She'd made a nest in the basement, a little nook for her litter of kittens." She shrugged, almost seeming embarrassed to prove she didn't have a cold heart, like being soft would ruin her tough image. "I was surprised the door wasn't locked. And when I made my deliveries, I'd bring her some milk and food and stuff. Brought a blanket, too."

"Why not just take them to the shelter?"

"Because they charge you fifty bucks to drop off a stray! Isn't that insane? It's not *my* cat. I just found her."

I smiled.

"What?" she asked, seeming guarded about my reaction.

"You and Yasmin. Similar in that you're cat people."

She rolled her eyes. "If it was a dog and puppies, same thing. I guess I related to her."

"Yasmin?" A bond over loving animals? That seemed basic, like part of human nature.

"No." She deadpanned. "The mama cat. Reminded me of myself. A mom without anyone to help. Being a mom on her own."

"What happened to Bree's dad?" It seemed risky to ask, but she seemed open this far.

"Yasmin happened to him," she sneered. "She stole Jasper from me in high school. I was with him first. I loved him first."

Whoa.

"He never acknowledged Bree as his kid. Sure, he'd pay child support, but he never acknowledged her, for fear of offending Yasmin. Yasmin pretended Bree didn't exist."

"That's...harsh." Fleetingly, I wondered if I was a hypocrite saying that. Here I was, warning my ex and his mom to leave Ella alone. But it was apples to oranges. Those people were a negative influence in my daughter's life.

"She denied that Bree could be Jasper's because she wanted him. Wanted this cute little high school sweetheart story with him. To be happily ever after."

"I'm sorry to hear that," I said honestly. "Families sure can be a mess."

"Family." Alexa scoffed. "What family? My sister betrayed me, calling me a liar and shunning me. She refused to believe he could have wanted her sister, even for a moment. Bree's been waiting her whole life for Jasper to pay attention to her, to be the dad she's always wanted."

I winced.

"Yasmin wasn't my sister, nope. No. She ceased being my sister when she cast me, cast her niece out of her life. I learned to let it go. She no longer mattered to me, but my girl? Bree has *hated* that woman all her life because she was the one thing standing in her way of having a daddy. Of having a 'family' like she always wanted."

I swallowed hard. That was a bold thing to say about a murdered woman.

"And if Yasmin wasn't there, Jasper might be available to be a family as Bree wanted?" I asked carefully.

Alexa narrowed her eyes at me. "Are you seriously thinking *Bree* killed her?"

It hadn't crossed my mind until now, but…
How can I not think that after what you said?

Chapter Twenty-Four

"Bree?" Alexa demanded. "You want to start a rumor that my *daughter* killed Yasmin?"

I raised my hands in a calm-down motion.

"For Pete's sake." She growled to the sky. "She didn't kill. Jeez. She's a kid! A teenager. I raised her better than to think about being violent. My God."

"I didn't actually think that," I said, backing up mentally. "But come on. If you heard what you said…"

Alexa shook her head. "So I spoke ill of the dead. I spoke ill of her when she was alive, too. Karma can come for me if it wants. That doesn't change the fact that Yasmin ruined our lives."

"What a mess," I said, for the lack of anything more constructive to add.

"Besides, he's with Melissa now. Or they're on and off. She hates pets and he loves his dogs. Who knows how *that* will work out. And Bree's going to get into that travel cheer camp. I know she will. When she does, she'll get picked up by a scout. I'm counting down the days until we can leave Fayette. She'll go pro, and I'll follow her to support her." She gestured at me. "Like you are doing, relocating with your Emma."

"Ella," I corrected.

"I'm not trying to put down Fayette. It's an all-right place to raise a kid." She tipped her head toward the neighbors. "Barb and Ingrid are cool ladies, if too nosy."

As we glanced toward the house next door, a car drove by, seeming to slow on this end of the neighborhood. Higher up on the porch, I had a clear vantage to watch the driver hang his arm out the open window as he surveyed the houses he passed, almost like scoping the area. In the passenger seat, a girl turned up the music obscenely loud and then cozied up to him, kissing him up as he drove.

Alexa growled lowly, and I was shocked to see that deep anger creasing her face again as she squinted at the car.

I glanced back, noticing a large decal on the rear window, proclaiming *CHR4EVER.*

"Was that Bree's car?"

Alexa faced me again, still upset, but not at me, it seemed. "Yeah, it was. Reminding me again why I'm eager to get out of here. If for nothing else than to get my baby girl away from that lazy, lying boyfriend of hers." She rolled her eyes, and I smiled, ever so grateful Ella wasn't boy-crazy.

"Who?" I asked. I hadn't seen the driver long enough to truly tell.

"Mark. Good-for-nothing, I tell you."

I remembered him. Ella's opinion of him and then that PleaseFundMe he'd set up when he quit his job. "Mark Varga," I said.

"Uh-huh. Melissa's brother. I never minded her, not really. Even if she did act like a snob when she won that lotto."

I raised my brows. "And even though she is with Jasper?"

"Nah. I made my peace with him long ago, as in I pretended he didn't exist. Sometimes, unrequited love *does* fade. And when it does, boy, you feel so dumb, wondering why you were infatuated for nothing good."

"You hated Yasmin for stealing Jasper, but you don't hate Melissa for having him now?" I asked.

"It's none of my business what he does now. He paid support for Bree. She's almost an adult now. It was Yasmin who did us dirty—extra dirty. She should have stood by me, her sister, her only family. Our parents died when we were young, so all we ever had was each other. Her not acknowledging Bree hurt more than when he didn't because I saw very quickly he was only avoiding Bree *for* Yasmin. Jasper only avoided Bree *because* of what Yasmin wanted. He was a puppet. A spineless puppet doing her wishes."

She switched again, gum to the other cheek and the mailbag to the opposite hip. "Bree doesn't hate Melissa either, I don't think. I'd say as she grew up and lost those childhood dreams, she understood it all."

And you probably shared your opinions about Jasper so much that she parroted them.

"And she's got other things on her mind now." Alexa's huff spoke of exhaustion. "Boys and all, you know?"

I didn't, actually. Again, I was so glad Ella cared more about being smart than being in love.

"I don't want Bree making the same excuse I did—falling for a hopeless cause like I did with Jasper at her age."

Chapter Twenty-Five

My thoughts about Alexa sure had changed with her sharing some backstory. I wasn't ready to call the woman a friend—she was too quick to be abrasive. While I didn't pity her for the cards life dealt her, I could relate almost. Being a single parent was no joke. It was a difficult battle to hang on to sanity parenting a teenager solo, too.

Underneath that antagonism and residual anger Alexa—and Bree—seemed to hang on to, I could sense that she wasn't an awful person deep down. Anyone who would go out of their way to take care of stray kittens had to be trustworthy at a basic level of human decency.

"I'll bet that's why Yasmin was there," I mumbled to myself as I left our house and walked over to Barbara and Ingrid's.

"What's that?" Ingrid asked as she brought her mail inside.

"Yasmin. She was at the historic founder's house because of cats."

She raised her brows as I entered the house. "Barbara and Ella went to the store. I was so confused, thinking I had the wrong measurements for the shelving. But they just had different packages compared to what I saw online." She shook her head. "They went to get the paint I ended up forgetting about."

I told her about what Alexa said, explaining how I figured the stray mama cat crying must have lured Yasmin closer.

"I didn't see any cat or kittens down there when Gin and I…" I winced.

Ingrid patted my back. "And you were likely shocked at what you *did* see, so much you wouldn't have noticed animals."

"Wonder if Chief Mooney or Officer Donn would have spotted them as they checked the area."

She raised her brows. "We could drive by and check. At least look for the window where the cat could have gotten in."

I slanted her a dubious look. "You're that eager to scope it out?"

She shrugged. "Adam said they were done with the scene. It'll have to be professionally cleaned, but they laid tarps over the mess."

"I still don't think we should just go traipsing around there…" I said, feeling like the voice of reason even though she was easily twice my age. "The chief already made a comment about me just happening to be at crime scenes."

She laughed heartily. "Oh, come on. We'll just look in the windows, not go *in* the basement." Pointing at the window, she said, "Besides, didn't you want to return that moving van before your bill is too high? It's just sitting there. How about I follow you to drop it off, and then on the way back, we'll swing by that historic building."

I twitched my mouth from side to side. "Well…okay."

On the drive to the franchise rental van company, I followed up with the texts Gin sent. He had a few appointments within the next couple of days, but he'd be able to show me his nephew's car after the last one.

"I guess I don't really *need* to go anywhere yet," I told Ingrid as she drove us through town. "It'll take a while to settle in, and with the furniture coming soon, I'll be too busy setting it all up to go anywhere."

"I love helping with furniture! IKEA manuals make me happy. So…to the point."

I laughed. "Good to know. But I should stock up the fridge." I glanced out the window, chuckling at myself. "I don't even know where it is yet!"

"There is a Walmart about ten miles away, but you can find the basic necessities at the grocery store at the end of Main. We can stop there on our way back to the house if you'd like."

I shrugged. "Sure. Thanks." That way, she could give me pointers on where what was. I never liked to browse through aisles looking for things. Too easy to give in to the many impulse buys that struck my fancy.

Unlike when Gin and I pulled up to the back of the building yesterday, Ingrid claimed a curb spot right in front of the historic founder's building. We scoped the street, smiling and waving at the cautious Miss Bellette when she peered out the window of her dry-cleaning place.

We'd found one window that looked like it had been recently patched up. Shiny new duct tape sealed a thick square of tarp to one end of the pane.

As we returned to Ingrid's car, I shrugged. "Maybe Officer Donn found the cats and taped up the hole."

"Mooney would have taken them to the shelter. Or Adam would have had one of his forensic techs see that they were cared for," Ingrid said, agreeing.

She got behind the wheel, and I climbed into the passenger seat. As I reached out to close my door, though, I caught sight of someone on the second-floor balcony. Smoke wafted up and the brightness of a cigarette flaring pulled my attention to the person standing out there.

"What?" Ingrid asked me, noticing that I hadn't closed the door yet.

"Hang on," I said, closing the door and opening the window. Ingrid cranked up the heat to compensate for my window being open. I pressed my lip to my mouth to indicate we should be quiet.

Melissa paced on the balcony, puffing on a cigarette as she spoke on her phone. Bundled in a puffy coat, she seemed protected from the weather, but it had to be chillier up high.

"I'm not giving you any money!" she shouted angrily. "I'm not giving *anyone* any more money." She scoffed. "Why? *Why*? Because it's *my* money and I don't have to give you any no matter how close we are."

Ingrid and I shared a look. *Whoa.*

"What I do is none of your business. You got that?" she sassed at whoever she was arguing with.

"And if anyone asks again, I'm not going to lie. I'm done covering for you." The laughter she followed that up with was an ugly sound. "I owe you? I don't owe you anything. You're just lucky no one's thought to check if you were actually here that night. But if someone brings it up again, I'm coming clean. I'm done with your problems."

Someone cleared their throat. Someone close to Ingrid's car. I jerked back when that someone rapped knuckles against the passenger door.

Roxana stepped up closer, her brows up as she studied us. "Eavesdropping, ladies?" she sneered. "Look who's trespassing on *my* property now, huh?"

Chapter Twenty-Six

Ingrid recovered faster than I did at Roxana catching us eavesdropping red-handed.

"*Your* property?" she taunted. "You just rent this place."

I frowned, raising a finger. "Wait. I heard you don't even pay rent. You just mooch off Melissa."

She gasped, dropping her mouth. "Who told you that? I pay her a little bit when I can."

"And we're on the street," Ingrid added. "Public property where anyone can be and listen to anything they please."

Roxana scowled, lunging forward to reach through the window.

I saw her coming, so I opened the door to block her from being able to reach in. She clearly intended to harm me somehow, or physically intimidate us. The doorframe smacked into her arm and chest, and she growled, teeth clenched. "You nosy, pestering idiots!"

I slammed the door shut as she rubbed her upper arm.

"If you don't want everyone to know secrets about covering up and lying, suggest she stay off the balcony while shouting then!" Ingrid said, already speeding away.

I scrambled to buckle, glancing in the mirror as Roxana ran inside the building. "Wow!"

Ingrid huffed. "Yeah. Wow is right."

"I didn't even notice Roxana on the sidewalk."

"Me neither. I was too busy listening in." At the red light, Ingrid shook her head. "I thought Melissa was talking *to* Roxana on the phone."

"Me too! Because it's not much of a secret she's wanting money and hurting for it." I frowned, putting the window back up. "And how come Roxana got into Melissa's good graces? It sounds like she's frugal with who she gives money to, but she lets Roxana mooch for rent?"

"I don't know. They were friends way back since they were kids. And Roxana used to smoke too, so I think she's the only one who is willing to put up with Melissa not kicking that habit."

"Hmm."

"Now what's interesting is Jasper does *not* smoke. His father passed away from lung cancer—a lifelong smoker—and Jasper's always been firmly anti-smoking. *That's* why I always assumed they never moved in together. He can't stand her smoking."

How would they even hook up or date then? He never kisses her, avoiding smoker breath? I shook my head. "Maybe that was who she was talking to, Jasper."

"He's always been hoping for a get-rich-quick opportunity," Ingrid said.

"Perhaps that's why he's seeing Melissa at all then."

Ingrid laughed, pulling up to the grocery store on Main as it wasn't far from this side of town. "Nah. She's not as loaded as it may sound like. Sure, she got a big influx of cash from the lotto. But she's spent a lot. And it wasn't much. Think hundreds of thousands, not mega-millions or billions."

I followed Ingrid inside and she waited as I grabbed a cart. It was a mini-cart, kind of cute and it offered a promising thought. Maybe I would be limited from impulse purchases of snacks I wanted to try but likely would never finish simply because not much space was available in the cart.

"Here's what I got from that though," Ingrid said. "Something I'll be calling Adam about."

I grinned. "I know you said he was never your beau, but you sure do stay in touch with him often."

"Oh, hush. Don't let Barbara think you're another cupid. He's a friend. I do talk to him often because I walk his dogs quite often when he's stuck working too much or on vacation. He's the county coroner, so he's spread thin."

"Ah." I picked up milk, butter, and eggs.

"We play poker once a week, too. So we're good friends, yes. And with Yasmin's body next door, it makes sense we're talking, well, I guess talking 'shop' a lot lately."

"Anyway, what do you need to tell him then?"

"Well, him and the chief. It seems she's hiding something, and I'd bet it has to do with Yasmin's murder."

I nodded as we entered the bread section. "I got that impression as well. Not only that, but she might be lying about an alibi."

Ingrid shook her head at my choice of bagels. "Those are on sale on Mondays," she advised. "Just wait and get them cheaper. But that's the odd thing. She *wasn't* talking to Roxana on the phone. And I recall that Roxana's alibi was verified by Melissa. And vice versa."

"Then...someone else. I agree, though. You should chat with them."

As we went down the aisle and then rounded to the next, I blinked in surprise. "Ella?"

Barbara and Ella seemed to be deep in a debate about ice cream. Ingrid laughed, and we caught up. "Funny running into you here."

"We wanted a cold snack for after painting," Barbara said.

"Yeah, Mom. The house is still hot. I guess it'll take a while for the heat to escape."

We joined our selections, the contents of their basket into my small cart, and it wasn't too long before the mini-cart looked full. As we shopped, Ingrid whispered with Barbara and Ella, telling them about what we'd just heard Melissa arguing about.

"I'll call Mike as soon as we get out of here," Barbara stated. I agreed. The chief should know—even if we'd obtained this news from eavesdropping. At the least, he should ask her about alibis again.

Lo and behold, when it was time to check out, we got into line right behind Jasper, whose card was declined.

"Sorry," he said shyly. "I thought I'd have a little more to pay down on that card."

Ingrid and I shared a knowing look. *Yep. There's no hiding the fact this man wishes he had more money. And might have been counting on getting some soon.*

"Been trying to kick that dang gambling habit once and for all…" He rubbed his hand over his hair.

I didn't get the sense he was fibbing. He truly looked embarrassed. On the conveyor belt, I saw stacks of wet cat food.

Oh, gosh. He's buying food for Yasmin's cats.

"Oh, hey. I'll get it."

His eyes bugged out. "Really?"

The cashier also looked at me wide-eyed. She scanned one can. Almost five bucks for a one-ounce can of slop? *Jeez.* I pasted on a bright, quick smile as I did the math. *Four and three-quarters times nine...* I widened my smile to hide any trace of regret that might slip over my face. *Yikes, was that more than I planned to spend.* "Sure. Sure."

"Oh, thanks. Ms. Front," Jasper gushed, smiling in relief. "I'll pay you back. Promise."

I won't hold my breath.

"I hadn't budgeted for these, you know." He shrugged, frowning at the cans. "Moopsy and Ferdinand—"

"Who?" Ella asked.

"My dogs," he clarified. "They sure don't like Winona and Rainbow Rain—Ray-Ray—moving back in but I was worried those poor cats would be abandoned. I got in touch with a cat show assistant Yasmin knew. She said she'll take the cats in but she can't drive out here to Fayette until next week. And Winona and Ray-Ray sure have a selective palette."

Not to mention expensive. What do they put in those teeny cans? Filet mignon?

"It's sweet of you to see after her cats though," Barbara said.

Jasper shrugged, nodding halfheartedly.

"Especially at the cost of Melissa's wrath."

He shook his head, scowling absently as the clerk continued to scan my purchases. "Oh, she'll never move in. She doesn't want to quit smoking. She was so jealous that I'd once shared the house with Yasmin. She hates my pets…"

I cleared my throat. "Well, you did say she's a passionate woman."

He grunted. "That's nonsense. Calling her 'passionate' is an excuse. To be polite. There's no denying she's just, well, mean! And if that's the case, she can just stay at the fancy apartment. Maybe Roxana will get off my back about it too."

"How so?" I asked, already suspecting what he'd say.

"She was threatened Mel would move in with me once and for all, and she can't afford that nice place on her own." He sighed, shaking his head. "You know, Yasmin and I weren't good for each other. I won't lie. We never should have married. But…I miss her. She was never *this* complicated, not with me."

The cashier, quiet until now, murmured agreement. "I miss her too."

Ella raised her face from looking at her phone. "You were close with Yasmin?"

"Well, sure. Everyone in Fayette knew her. She was a steady customer, specifically requesting we order that outrageously expensive brand of food." She pointed a long, hot-pink nail at the cans at the end of the conveyor belt.

Jasper winced, and I smiled at him. "Hey, for a good cause. My good deed for the day."

"But I'll miss her," the cashier continued. "She might not have known *how* to express her concerns, maybe sounded kinda like a"—she rolled her eyes and sighed heavily— "'Karen.'"

Ella giggled, and I had to smile at the irony. The cashier's nametag read *Caryn*.

"And Yasmin mighta butted into everyone's business, but sometimes the world needs those kinda people. You know? She kept people on their toes. She posted pics of that lady who kept speeding by the school, shared pics of her license plate. Bam. Mr. Donn and Mr. Mooney caught her speeding *and* there's gonna be a speed bump now. Same with the old dude who liked to do a rolling stop at the stop sign by the library. He nearly hit my boy when he was biking, and she struck again. She shamed him online with a pic of him not braking, and he stopped doing it."

"Caryn," another employee said. "I'll open up lane two, all right?"

I looked to see we had a line forming as Caryn took her time scanning my many items. *Guess you can pack quite a bit in that little cart.*

"She posted about that creep who kept catcalling my niece during her soccer practice, and boom, he was suspended. The world needs a watchful eye."

"I think *every*one should look out for others," Barbara said.

"And Yasmin mighta lacked tact, but she was good under it all." Caryn wiped at her eyes. "I checked her out that day she was killed, you know. Came in here and bought a bunch of cat food. I was curious why she didn't get her usual expensive stuff. She said generic was fine for the strays she found nearby."

Aww. She had *been there taking care of the strays.*

"Of course, she complained about having to pay to drop them off, so she'd let someone else find them and pay that fee." Caryn rolled her eyes. "She was as cheap and as much of a penny pincher as anyone else. Still, she did Fayette a service." She leaned, setting her hand on the conveyor belt to talk directly to us, my purchases all rung up. I winced at the total.

"She was all giddy to drop some food to those strays and hurry home. Excited to post a picture about someone breaking into Mr. Gaelean's house. She caught that thief sneaking out with a big old handful of jewelry! Says he ran from her when she spotted him while walking Ray-Ray."

Jasper shook his head. "No. Ray-Ray was allergic to grass. She walked Winona."

Caryn deadpanned at him. "Whichever. She says the thief ran off, calling her a nosy, well, a bad name. So, she was excited to post a picture of him and shame him too!"

"Oh, no!"

We turned at the gasp. A teen looked pale and stricken, clasping a pendant at her neck. "He didn't. He—oh, no. He *stole* it?" She gaped, looking at the glittering gems on the necklace she lifted from her chest. "Oh, *no...*"

She ran out, and Ella gawked, pointing.

"El," Barbara scolded, shoving her hand down. "Not nice to point."

"That was—"

Ingrid straightened, seeming to connect something faster than I could. "Bree!"

Alexa's daughter? I clearly wasn't thinking fast enough. *The one who dated...*

"She's his girlfriend. You saw her freaking out about that necklace she had on. That huge, expensive necklace. I just bet Mark stole it and gave it to her!" Ella said.

"And if Mark knew Yasmin had incriminating evidence of his *latest* crime," Ingrid said.

Barbara pulled out her phone. "I'm calling. I'm calling. No matter what he says about butting out of others' business and staying out of his case…"

"He's just mad you can solve them faster than he does!" Ingrid said, rushing out of the store.

"What's… What's going on?" Jasper asked, watching Ingrid, then Barbara running out of the store.

"Mom, I bet Melissa was talking to Mark."

I nodded at Ella as we hurried to bag all our things.

Jasper still seemed clueless. "Mark's her younger brother."

I thought back to what Ingrid and I overheard.

"I don't have to give you any no matter how close we are." She'd been talking about giving someone money to someone close to her. Not as a friend or lover, but a relative.

I glanced outside, worried about Ingrid and Barbara dashing out there.

"If Melissa threatened Mark that she wouldn't cover for his alibi anymore…" I gulped, catching Ella's worried frown.

"What's to say he won't try to silence her so she can't tell the truth?" Ella wondered aloud.

AUBREY ELLE

Chapter Twenty-Seven

"What's going on?" Jasper asked, helping Ella and me hurry to bag the things.

"Mark's got to be going after Melissa," Ella said.

"That's ridiculous. She's his sister." He huffed bitterly. "The hand that feeds."

"She lied about his alibi, and she's going to come clean," I said.

"You're jumping to conclusions," Jasper said. "Mark lives there, too. She said he was at home, in the apartment downstairs."

When Ella and I didn't comment, grabbing as many bags as we could carry out, Jasper frowned and took the remaining bags. "Are you sure? You really think she's in danger?"

As we exited, I saw Ingrid's car was gone.

"Barbara has the keys," Ella cried out at the car parked further down the street.

"You think Melissa's in danger?" Jasper said. "Mark is a danger?"

A police car zoomed by, lights on.

I frowned, glancing at where the historic founder's building was. "They're going the wrong way."

"Come on." Jasper jogged to a clunker of a Jeep that had seen better days. "I'll drive. Hurry!"

We rushed over and climbed in. The bags barely fit, crammed into the back with Ella, well, they would survive.

Melissa might not.

A couple of bobbleheads danced on the dashboard as Jasper pulled from the curb, executed an illegal turn, and sped toward Melissa's building.

"Barbara was already on the phone." I held on to the *oh no* bar at his rough driving. "If I call 911, I don't want to interrupt whatever call she's already on."

"We'll be there in a minute," Jasper promised, worry on his face. "Melissa's no good for me, but my gosh, no one should be murdered!"

He parked haphazardly in less than a minute. I sure hoped he was wrong. If we were jumping to the wrong conclusions and he'd just sped through town for no reason, I'd feel terrible.

"They're here." Ella got out, pointing at Ingrid's car.

"Hold on. No point in all of us entering a dangerous situation," I told Ella, blocking her from running inside.

"Exactly," Jasper said, blocking *me* back, too.

A scream sounded from the back, and we all ran.

Miss Bellette lay on the ground, Ingrid helping her up.

"She fainted. I just came here as he slipped into the basement. He was holding a gun, and she got scared, and just—" Ingrid shook her head.

"Mark went down there?" Jasper nodded at the basement access to the building.

Barbara jogged closer, her phone to her ear. "Dispatch says they're out at a semi-truck accident near the highway. They're coming." She cowered back by Ingrid helping to sit up Miss Bellette. "Mark ran back there just as we snuck up from the front. Roxana was leading Melissa down there. After Mark darted down, Bree rushed down, too!"

Jasper took off.

"Here, help her," Ingrid said to Barbara, helping to shift Miss Bellette to her lap.

Then she took off too.

Ella gasped. "She can't— They can't just— They can't just run in there!"

Sirens sounded too far away.

"Oh, Ingrid's no weakling."

She had served in the Army. As a nurse. Still, I feared for her rushing into danger.

"Ella, stay here." I stood and ran toward them too.

"Mom!" she called after me from the distance. "What the heck are you doing?"

It didn't matter that we'd only met. I couldn't stand by and let Ingrid run into danger.

Friends don't let friends risk themselves.

And I would never forgive myself if something happened to her while I stood around waiting for help!

Chapter Twenty-Eight

Ingrid crouched at the door basement door, peeking in, her phone on and recording. She frowned at me, shushing me out of sight from those in the basement.

Down below, Jasper clutched Bree in a hug, shielding her from Mark, who held a gun at them all.

Roxana aimed a knife at Melissa, who sported a swollen eye and a furious scowl.

"Some dirty trick, telling me you wanted to show me some new lock pad the landlord installed after the chief released the scene," Melissa said. She spat a mouthful of blood to the ground.

"If you would've just cooperated and given me some more money like I asked, I would have been able to leave town." Mark paced, shifting his gun from being trained on one person then the next.

"Safety's not even off," Ingrid mouthed to me, nodding at the gun.

That explained why she didn't seem more worried.

"I bet he doesn't even know how to use it. Holding it wrong," she added quietly as we crouched in the stairwell, watching.

"No!" Melissa shouted. "I'm done giving you money. I'm done hearing you beg for money and wanting everything handed to you."

"You were supposed to give us thirds!" Roxana snarled. "All three of us gave you numbers for that winning ticket."

"So. What! I *bought* the ticket. I *chose* the numbers in the end. I don't owe either of you murderers anything!" Melissa said.

"I never killed anyone," Roxana said.

"But you're the one who helped him hide her!" Melissa shouted. "You're the one who used a blanket to move her after he lost his temper and killed her."

"It was an accident," Mark said, rubbing his head.

"Oh, sure." Melissa rolled her eyes. "You *accidentally* stabbed her. Three times. That's a lie. You wanted her to shut up before she shared that picture of you stealing stuff. I'm done with it all. I'm not going to lie and say you were all at home. I'm through with you all!"

"If you hadn't freaked out," Mark said, "I could have left her here and no one would have found her to begin with."

"I'm not going to live somewhere with a corpse nearby in storage!" Melissa shrieked.

I tried not to take insult at that.

"This is *your* mess," Melissa said. "And I'm done with you."

Roxana held up the knife at her face. "You sure about that? You think you can call the shots right now?"

"Melissa." Mark shook his head. "Just give me the money so I can leave town until this blows over."

"No, please don't go," Bree cried out. "I don't want to lose you."

"Oh, shut up!" Mark yelled, aiming the gun at her.

"Don't talk to my daughter like that!" Jasper shouted.

"Shut up!" Mark repeated.

"I'm not giving you money, and I'm not lying about anyone's alibis anymore!" Melissa said.

"We'll see about that," Roxana said. "Your lie can just die with you!"

She lunged for Melissa with the knife, and everyone reacted.

Jasper burst forward, knocking Roxana to the ground. Melissa stood to run, but she tripped over Jasper lying atop Roxana as he wrestled to smack the knife away. Mark pointed his gun at all of them on the ground, but he dropped the firearm when he tried to figure out the safety.

Just in time for Officer Donn and Chief Mooney to show up, shouting at Ingrid and me to back up and get out of the way.

We flattened ourselves to the stairwell wall so they could pass.

Rolling our heads to face each other, we grinned.

"Case closed, I'd say," Ingrid said.

"My thoughts exactly," I said breathlessly. *And in the nick of time, just before anyone could get hurt again.*

Ingrid lingered at the basement entrance, speaking with a cop as they took charge of the almost-crime scene. Breathing easier that the suspense was over, I returned to Ella and Barbara who comforted a now-awake Miss Bellette. I couldn't understand much of her broken English and French mixture, but I couldn't really hear her either. Ella scolded me for running after Ingrid.

"You wouldn't let *me* run into danger like that," she said, hugging me tightly.

"Because *I'm* your mother. *I'm* the adult."

Barbara narrowed her eyes at me. "Hmmm. That's no argument."

"You didn't seem worried."

"Because Ingrid has training. Expired, long-ago training, but she's witnessed combat and danger firsthand from being in the service. I knew she'd keep you safe. And herself."

Feels like we just got lucky.

We waited at the dry cleaners as a paramedic assisted the frail young lady to fully regain consciousness. On the sidewalk, I couldn't help but think it was repeating itself all over again.

Ella and I standing outside a crime scene, chilly in the cold. Only this time, Barbara stood with us, not next door and beckoning us into a warm kitchen.

Ingrid eventually walked over, chatting and laughing with a cop.

"I'll bet Mike's busy at the moment," Barbara said when Ingrid neared us.

"Yeah, he's got it under control," the officer said.

When Ingrid reached us, she sighed and then smiled. "Eager to gloat *you* solved his case before he could?"

"Oh, you better believe it." Barbara winked at us. "For all those times he's scolded me about butting out of other people's business and minding my own…"

"This time," I said. Surely we didn't move in next to a pair of true sleuths.

Looking at me, then Ella, and lastly, Barbara, Ingrid raised a brow and proposed, "How about a nice pot of Rose Raspberry to help us calm down from all this excitement, then?"

Ella barked out a laugh. "Is there ever a situation when you *don't* think tea is the solution?"

Barbara slung her arms around my shoulders and hers. "Eh. If you ask me, a nice pot of hot tea solves any spell of trouble life can throw at us."

And as the sirens blared on, the lights flashing against the old walls of the founder's building and Miss Bellette's dry cleaning shop, we headed home.

Chapter Twenty-Nine

One month later…

Sporting a hard hat, goggles, and a dust mask, Ella stepped up to the shed. She hefted a sledgehammer up high and swung it into a post that once held up the shed. Ingrid and I had torn down most of the walls. The roof had fallen in during a burst of heavy snow followed by a super-fast, unusually warm spring day. As the snow melted and sank the roof, it gave way.

Barbara and I stood near a fire pit, rubbing our gloved hands in the warmth. Ingredients for s'mores waiting on a table Ingrid and Barbara had gifted us as a home-warming present—a patio set that they figured was more of a selfish purchase since they planned to be invited over often.

Their home was ours, they'd claimed, and it went without saying Ella and I welcomed them here. There was no denying their eccentric home was more interesting, though.

In the weeks after the conclusion of Yasmin's murder case, Ella and I had fallen into a little bit of a better routine. She was still a grouch waking up for school mornings. I was enjoying my job as a secretary—so far. I wondered if it was a honeymoon phase yet, and I'd eventually hit a lull like I imagined most people did with a steady job.

"Maybe a little more cinnamon is needed?" Barbara said of the Chai tea she'd brought over in a thermos for us to enjoy. It was an amusing guessing game she'd played with herself as she'd brainstormed what tea paired well with graham crackers, chocolate, and marshmallows.

"I like this just fine."

She scoffed. "Because you're the easiest person on the planet to please, Naomi."

I grinned. And pleased I was. New home, new friends, and a new job. Even better, no more Blane, no more dead bodies, and no more rickety eyesore of a shed.

Ella missed her swing, spinning with the momentum.

"You gotta hit it like a baseball," Barbara called.

"Organized sports are a waste of time," Ella sassed. "They promote unrealistic expectations of the youth's physique and promote competition that borders on—"

"Okay, okay," Ingrid said, clapping her hands almost like she *was* a coach of said sport. "Eye on the ball. I mean, eye on the board."

Since the roof had fallen in, I figured it wouldn't be too much to tear the rest of the shed down. I'd already scoured the hardware stores for the model I wanted to purchase. Glancing at the opposite corner of the backyard, I squinted at the glare of Mrs. West's TV. The garish neon and flashes from dark to bright rivaled the glow of the fire in the pit.

"Maybe in March, the ground will thaw enough to set up a new one?" I guessed.

"Eh. It can still be winter then. Depends on Mother Nature's mood," Barbara said.

"What's this I hear about loud crashes and bangs?" a man called from the driveway.

Chief Mooney ambled up, his hands in his pockets.

"Oh, no one called in a complaint about noise," Barbara said.

"Wanna bet?" her cousin replied.

Ella hit the beam. It cracked and crashed another portion of the low wall down.

"Really?" I asked. "I'm sorry."

He shrugged. "Looks like you're almost done, anyhow." Then he tipped his chin in the direction of Mrs. West's house. "I'll let your 'noise' be payback for all the complaints we've received about the 'light pollution' from that huge TV she never shuts off."

Joining us at the fire, he held his hands out to warm them up. "I actually wanted to stop by for another reason."

"To say thank you for figuring out who killed Yasmin for you?" Barbara asked, her tone light and singsongy.

"No." He smirked at her.

"Were you even suspecting Mark?" I asked. I hadn't seen much of Fayette's law enforcement since they'd come to the founder building's basement. And boy, did they arrive just in time.

It was a blessing Mark was inept at handling a gun because it sure could have gone worse.

"Yes. And no. The catch was he had an alibi— same as Roxana's actually, in that they were both tenants at that building with Melissa." He shook his head. "The stupid mistake she had of lying for them. Especially after knowing they would go to the extremes of actually killing someone and hiding them!"

"Maybe she lied for them because she was afraid of them," Ella said.

"And admitting she was afraid of anyone or anything wasn't something Melissa wanted to do, it seems." The chief stepped closer yet, seeking the fire pit's warmth.

"I still don't understand Roxana, though," Ella said.

She'd confessed that she'd helped Mark hide Yasmin's body since Melissa was *not* happy about a murder happening in the building she lived in. According to Roxana's testimony, she claimed she only helped Mark remove Yasmin's body because Melissa assumed Mark never would, and Yasmin would rot at her home. That Mark never followed through with what he said he'd do—a bona fide lazy liar to the core.

"What? Why she tried to kill Melissa?" I asked.

"To silence Melissa from fessing up about what she knew they did," Barbara said.

"No. Why Roxana was snooping around here after Yasmin was found." Ella left Ingrid at the shed, let the sledgehammer sink to the grass, and approached us at the fire. "She was looking for that receipt that proved she'd purchased those knives."

I nodded, sipping my tea.

"But the knife used to kill Yasmin wasn't Roxana's. It was a knife Mark stole when he quit the bakery."

Wilson Bakery—formerly Jameson Bakery, hence why I'd misunderstood. I'd thought from Mark's

PleaseFundMe posts about donations so he didn't have to work that Mark had quit working for a *person* named Jameson. I hadn't known that Wilson Bakery had just bought out Jameson Bakery.

"She thought she'd given Yasmin a different receipt," Chief Mooney said. "One she wanted back."

"Huh?" Barbara asked.

"Roxana testified that she ran into Yasmin in the back. Yasmin was there to check on the strays, and Roxana gave her a receipt for a camera. One she wanted Yasmin to pay for half of since she couldn't return it because the return date had passed. She'd kept the camera for herself, but she wanted compensation."

"Compensation where it wasn't due," I quipped.

He nodded. "She shoved the receipt at her, but Yasmin didn't want it. Then Roxana shoved it into her pocket and stormed off. Then Mark approached her to not post the pictures of him breaking into that house and stealing jewelry. She refused, so he killed her. Then Melissa was unhappy about it all and demanded he move her. But he didn't have a car, so he roped Roxana in to help since they used to hang out together."

"So, what, she later realized she'd given her a receipt for that knife set?" Ella asked.

"And worried that it could be taken as a clue when her body was found?" I guessed.

"Yep." Chief Mooney went over to the shed, picking up the sledgehammer. "That was it."

He took a swing and busted down a stubborn post that hadn't given up yet. "I do appreciate you ladies and your diligence to keeping Fayette as safe and crime-free as possible, but if I ever hear that you're running into a potentially dangerous scene like that again..." He swung the sledgehammer at another post and knocked it down. "Well, let's just agree that *won't* happen again, huh?"

None of us spoke.

"Because that could have turned out badly. A firearm, a knife, volatile tempers..." He sighed. "That's why I always tell you to *please* butt out of my cases, Barbara." His stern glare seemed intended for all of us.

"If I'd butted out and we hadn't sleuthed it out, you might not have been able to get there in time," Barbara retorted. "But it's all over with now," she tacked on cheerily.

"Mark's in jail, Roxana too. Melissa's charged with obstruction of justice, and Jasper got Yasmin's savings," Ingrid summed up.

"It's sweet of him to keep the cats when the cat show gal backed out," Barbara added. "Even sweeter when he apologized to Bree for never being there for her as she grew up. I doubt Alexa will ever forgive him, but it made me so happy to see him sitting with them at the café, owning up to never acknowledging her and apologizing for it."

Ella scoffed. "It's not like a simple sorry can erase a whole childhood of a guy being a bad dad."

I hugged her side, hating Blane even more for the sad tone in her voice.

"No," Barbara said. "But it was an honorable attempt to admit his fault."

"First time ever that he'd done *that*," Ingrid said. "Seeing Bree near Mark waving a gun around really must have shocked him into owning up to his stupidity about neglecting his daughter."

"Most of all, though," I said louder, wishing to get past the topic of lousy father figures for Ella's sake. And to avoid another scolding from Chief Mooney. "Life can now go on at a normal, ordinary pace with usual, typical events. No more surprises waiting to stump us and making us wonder what-ifs." I raised my mug of tea. "To a wonderful life in Fayette with the best of neighbors."

"Hear, hear," Barbara chimed in, clinking her cup to mine.

Ella and Ingrid joined in too, toasting to a peaceful fresh start for me and my daughter in this little town.

Chief Mooney simply stood there, leaning on the sledgehammer handle. He raised his finger, chuckling wryly as he pointed at me. "You better not have jinxed yourself there, Naomi."

Even if I had, and more trouble landed in our paths, I knew with Ella, Barbara, and Ingrid, I had a team of the best girls to support me along the way.

About the Author

Aubrey Elle is an author of cozy mysteries. While she also writes romantic suspense under the pen name of Amabel Daniels, *Mischief Over Mums* is her debut cozy novel, featuring a landscaper in a small town in Ohio. By day, Aubrey chases after her young daughters and tries to keep up with her own landscaping, and by night, she writes until the midnight hour. Aubrey lives with her family and many pets in Ottawa Hills, OH.

Want to stay connected?

Other Books by Aubrey Elle

Madis Harrah Mysteries

Mischief Over Mums

Tumultuous Time to Tulips

Protection by Petunias

Hold Up Hydrangeas

Danger Before Dahlias

Ring Gone 'Round the Roses Free short story!

Missteps in Murder

Peril at the Party

Death at the Dance

Bump at the Ball

Tea Time Troubles

A Spot of Earl Slay

Death and Deja Brew

Steeped in Murder

Made in the USA
Columbia, SC
01 August 2023

21123354R00155